GORDON KORMAN

BOOK TWO: SURVIVAL

ISLAND

AN
APPLE
PAPERBACK

SCHOLASTIC INC.
New York Toronto London Auckland Sydney
Mexico City New Delhi Hong Kong Buenos Aires

For Socrates and Krista Panageas

ISBN 0-439-16457-5

24 23 22 21 20 19 18 17 16 15 14 13 3 4 5 6/0

Printed in the U.S.A. 40

First Scholastic printing, July 2001

PROLOGUE

On the beach of the small coral island with no name sat all that was left of the schooner *Phoenix*. It was a tiny wooden raft, six feet long and not quite four feet wide, and had once been the roof over the proud ship's galley. Now it was scorched by fire, battered by weather, and encrusted with sand and sea salt. Barely visible through the battle scars were three letters: N-I-X. The rest of the *Phoenix*'s name, along with the ship herself, lay at the bottom of the deepest part of the Pacific Ocean.

On this piece of flotsam, four young people had braved seven days and nights at the mercy of the sea. Their captain was gone, drowned. The mate had deserted them, leaving them to die. Two of their companions were lost without a trace. Close to death from hunger, thirst, and the blazing sun, the four survivors had ridden the wind and waves. Three of them were in a desperate condition, the fourth deeply unconscious when they washed ashore on this rugged cay, six thousand miles west of Los Angeles, eleven hundred miles south of Tokyo, and nine hundred miles east of Hong Kong.

It was a tiny dot in the vast ocean, a dot that appeared on no maps, overlooked no shipping lanes, and was observed by no passing aircraft — an island with no name.

CHAPTER ONE

Day 1, 4:45 P.M.

They had survived forty-foot waves, an explosion and fire at sea, and a week adrift on a tiny raft. But now Luke Haggerty, Charla Swann, and Ian Sikorsky faced their greatest challenge so far:

A coconut.

It had fallen off a tall palm, missing Luke's ear by inches. To three people who had put nothing but rainwater in their stomachs for seven long days, it represented what they needed most: food.

Charla, the city kid, turned it over in her hands. "Where's the opener on this thing?"

"What do you expect?" Luke shot back. "A pull tab?"

It was a joke, but it underscored the tension and fear in the group. Will Greenfield, the fourth survivor, lay unconscious and unmoving on a beach not far away. He needed medical attention. Probably they all did. But they were far from any doctor or hospital, stranded on a — on a what? It had to be an island. But how big an island? And where? It was anybody's guess.

4

Be grateful, Luke reminded himself. *You're alive.*

But he was not grateful. Captain Cascadden wasn't alive. Lyssa Greenfield and J.J. Lane weren't alive. Luke felt their absence in his every breath, an overwhelming sadness that weighed on him as heavily as exhaustion and dehydration.

What was so special about Luke that he deserved to live when others had perished? Why was he still here?

Good luck?

Or maybe the luck wasn't so good after all. The hunger felt more powerful than death. Forget hunger pangs. Luke hadn't felt those in days. Instead, there was a grinding hollow emptiness where his stomach should have been. The sensation was so intense that it seemed to go outside the limits of his skin. With it came a nervous trembling weakness that was only going to get worse.

And here was this coconut . . .

"You have to break it," explained Luke, banging it on the damp ground. "You have to get through that tough skin." He snatched up a rock and began bashing it against the greenish shell. "It takes patience!" He picked it up and hurled it at a tree. "Open, you miserable, rotten — "

It bounced off with a thwack and hit the ground, unbroken.

Ian spoke up. "I once saw a documentary about native tribes who could crack coconuts with their bare hands."

"Did you bother to find out how they did it?" Luke asked irritably.

Ian shook his head. "That was in Part Two. They showed it the night I left for this trip."

The three exchanged a stricken look. It was hard to believe that, barely two weeks ago, they had been safe at home, packing for Charting a New Course, a monthlong boat excursion meant to help troubled youth.

Charla sounded slightly hysterical. "It's like starving to death at Thanksgiving dinner!" she cried. She picked up the fallen coconut, spun around, and hurled it like a discus into the jungle.

Crack!

"It broke!" exclaimed Ian. "I heard it!"

They rushed into the dense trees, but their coconut was nowhere to be seen. Vines and underbrush snatched at their legs.

Luke grabbed a branch and began hacking away at the tangle. The coconut! The *food*! It had to be down here somewhere! He began to flail wildly, like a crazed golfer in knee-deep rough.

He roared in anger; it was stupid, he knew — a waste of valuable energy when there was so little left. But his frustration mixed with his hunger, and he didn't care, couldn't help himself. . . .

"Luke!" Charla grabbed him from behind. "Stop it! It's only a coconut."

"Guys!" came Ian's excited voice. "Over here!"

They followed his call to a small grove of leafy tropical trees and shrubs. There the younger boy was gathering an armload of strange green fruits that had fallen to the ground.

Charla wrinkled her nose. "What stinks?"

"These are durians," Ian explained breathlessly. "They have a strong odor, but they're food." He broke one open against a tree trunk and handed half to Luke. The powerful smell tripled.

Luke stared at it. "You're kidding, right?" The thick skin was covered in spikes. It looked more like a deadly weapon than a fruit.

Charla accepted a piece, handling it as if it might explode. "But — how do we know it isn't poison?"

Ian plucked out a gigantic seed and began to eat the grayish mush around it. "There was this documentary on TV — " he began, mouth full.

Luke and Charla locked eyes. They had

learned from experience that Ian was never wrong about something he'd seen on television. His stockpile of knowledge had saved their lives more than once on the raft.

They fell on the offering like starving sharks. It wasn't good, Luke reflected. It wasn't even acceptable. But in his voracious hunger, he barely noticed, gorging himself on fruit the consistency of gritty pudding, but with an odd garlicky flavor. Back home, he wouldn't have given this stuff table room. But here he ate greedily, even crunching the rock-hard seeds because Ian said they needed the protein.

The feast soon turned into a frenzy. After no food for so long, once they started eating, they couldn't stop themselves. The three stumbled around the grove in a fever of appetite, tripping and falling over the dozens of discarded rinds even as they rushed to break open new fruit. The rough spikes scratched their knees and shins, yet none of them felt the sting. Nothing mattered, nothing but the breathless race to get on the outside of as much nourishment as humanly possible.

As he stuffed himself, at long last Luke could feel his stomach again, back where it belonged and comfortably full. The sensation came along with something unexpected — sudden, overpowering sleepiness. All at once, his eyelids were so heavy that he couldn't keep them from closing.

Drowsy panic. Had they poisoned themselves?

The others must have experienced it too. Just before he lost consciousness, he heard Charla say, "God, what did we eat? I can't stay awake!"

Seconds later, the three of them lay motionless, the remnants of their feast still scattered around them.

CHAPTER TWO

Day 1, 10:50 P.M.

Locker inspection.

It flashed before Luke's eyes in a series of still pictures: The assistant principal flipping through his untidy collection of books and sneakers. A pause to wave those sweaty gym shorts to everybody in the hall — the guy was a real comedian. And then . . .

A small hard shape in his wadded-up backpack; stubby fingers drawing it out — a thirty-two-caliber pistol.

"It's not mine, Mr. Sazio!"

Even now, lying unconscious in the jungle of a deserted island nine thousand miles away, Luke protested his innocence.

"Somebody framed me!"

And just like it had happened in real time, he was not believed.

The rush began: the trial, the choice — six months in Williston Juvenile Detention Facility, or a program called CNC — Charting a New Course. Four weeks of sailing aboard the *Phoenix*, a majestic schooner. There he would learn discipline, cooperation, and respect for law and order.

The images changed. He could hear the tremendous explosion, feel the hot wind of the blast on his face, see the approaching wall of fire. . . .

Something snuffled, and it wasn't an explosion. Luke awoke with a start. It was so dark that, for an instant, he thought he was back on the raft. A sliver of moon provided the only light.

Then he saw the creature. It was just a few inches away, staring back at him with glowing red eyes.

Luke gasped in shock and revulsion. Instinct told him to back up. But flat on the ground, he had nowhere to go.

The beast retreated a couple of steps, snorting and puffing. It was four feet long, seemingly all head and bull neck, with a body that tapered to short legs and a tail. On either side of the flat snout curled small gleaming white tusks that gave the animal the appearance of sporting a well-groomed mustache.

A boar! Luke thought. *A wild boar!* And he was lying here helpless. . . .

All in one motion, he rolled away and scrambled to his knees. The boar was startled and thundered into the jungle, its massive head pumping up and down like a piston as it ran.

Luke squinted around the clearing, making out the shapes of his two companions, still lying there asleep. At least, he *hoped* they were asleep. He stood up and felt a paralyzing cramp grip his stomach.

He doubled over and tried not to panic. "If it were poison, you'd be dead already," he told himself out loud.

They had eaten some very weird stuff — too much, too fast after a week of no food at all. That had to be a shock to the system, and Luke's stomach was letting him know it.

An itch on his cheek took his attention from his digestion. He reached up and scratched. Bumps. At least a dozen. Bug bites, all over his face. His eyelid was starting to swell. There were welts on his arms too, and the bare part of his legs below his ragged shorts. On his head, even, beneath his thick brown hair! While he'd been sleeping, he had provided a banquet for the local island insects. He could hear the buzzing in his ears. He flailed his arms, but the sound didn't go away.

Charla stirred and immediately curled into a ball. "Oh, my stomach! What was in that fruit? Cyanide?"

"I think we just overdid it," Luke groaned.

She was unconvinced. "Are you sure? I'm breaking out in a rash. I itch all over!"

"Bugs!" Luke exclaimed, slapping and swatting. All at once, a thought came to him that made him forget insects and stomach cramps. "Will!" he exclaimed in horror.

Ian sat bolt upright. "He's awake?"

"We just left him there on the beach!"

"Well," began Charla, working hard to sound calm, "it's not like he can go anywhere — "

"I saw a wild boar tonight," Luke said breathlessly. "It didn't hurt me, but Will can't defend himself. We've got to get back there!"

They ran through the dense brush, stumbling with heavy legs over the spaghetti of vines. Luke tried to will his feet to step higher, but he couldn't seem to summon the energy.

"Hold it! Hold it!" Charla grabbed him by the arm and stopped him. "Do you remember how to find the beach? I don't."

The three looked around, struggling to sharpen senses that were dulled by fatigue and discomfort. In the darkness, all directions seemed equally possible.

"I can't see it," Luke said finally. "I can barely see you guys."

"Be quiet," ordered Ian. "Now, what do you hear?"

"I hear mosquitoes, and lots of them!" moaned Charla. "Let's get out of here!"

"Listen to the silence," Ian insisted.

This time Luke fought the impulse to run from the insects that were devouring him. Instead, he forced himself to open his ears and mind. There was the buzzing, sure. Against a backdrop of nothing, it seemed as loud as a squadron of planes. But slowly, he became aware of other, quieter sounds — the scurrying of small nocturnal birds and animals; the rustle of the wind in palm fronds; and, over it all, a distant, rhythmic pounding.

His brain was working in slow motion, so there was a delayed reaction. "The surf!" he exclaimed finally.

Ian pointed. "This way!"

A few minutes later, they broke out of the trees. Running had served to clear their heads a little. Luke offered up a high five that Charla took a weak slap at. The celebration was short-lived.

An indentation in the soft sand showed the spot where Will had been lying.

Their friend was nowhere to be seen.

CHAPTER THREE

Day 1, 10:35 P.M.

When Will Greenfield finally regained consciousness, it was sudden, with a start. One moment he was in a faraway, dreamless place, and the next he was sitting up, awake, alert. Wired, even.

"Where am I?" His voice was hoarse, scratchy. Man, he was thirsty! Hungry too. And what a headache!

It was pitch-dark, but he could feel the sand beneath him and hear the ocean.

What was going on? Had he fallen asleep at the beach?

He tried to think, but he couldn't focus on anything past the pounding of his head and the relentless gnawing in his stomach. His brain was in a fog. He could almost see it — waves of silvery gray mist.

But mist shouldn't be visible in the blackness. . . .

Think! he ordered himself.

The last thing he remembered, he had been on the plane bound for Guam and Charting a New Course. His sister, Lyssa, got the extra peanuts and — big surprise — refused to share.

Peanuts. He sure could use some peanuts now. . . .

Forget the peanuts! Think!

Guam. This must be Guam! But what happened to Charting a New Course? And where was Lyssa?

His freckled features formed a nervous frown. His parents had sent him and his sister halfway around the world for CNC. The trip was supposed to teach them to get along. It was a huge deal to Mom and Dad — big money too. If he missed it, they'd never forgive him. Lyssa was already their little darling. That would only get worse if everybody was mad at him.

He felt white-hot rage. Lyssa did this! She set him up so he would miss the trip. Only — why couldn't he remember her doing it? Why couldn't he remember how he got here at all?

He stood up — muscles very stiff. How long had he been sleeping? Wait a minute — these weren't the clothes he'd been wearing on the plane! He was clad only in shorts and a T-shirt, both absolutely ruined.

Oh, Lyssa was going to pay for this one. . . .

He began to explore the beach — slowly; his feet were unsteady. He felt as if he might overbalance and fall flat on his face at any moment.

There was just enough light for him to make out the ocean on one side and a jungle of palm trees on the other. What he couldn't make out was anything else — no people, no buildings, nothing. Guam wasn't exactly New York City, but it was a place with towns, an airport, a marina where the *Phoenix*, CNC's boat, was supposed to be parked.

Not parked, he reminded himself. *Moored.*

He stopped in his tracks. How would he know something like that? He was totally clueless when it came to sailing.

"Will?" came a voice from the distance.

Lyssa?

No, the voice was male.

"Will, where are you?"

Now *that* one was definitely a girl.

"Lyssa?" He broke into a sprint. "Lyss, I don't know what kind of a joke you think this is — "

He pulled up short. Two boys and a girl were running across the beach, staring at him as if he'd just come back from the dead. Lyssa was nowhere to be seen.

"Who are you?" demanded Will. "Where's my sister?"

They froze, eyes widening.

The first boy — the leader? — took a cautious step forward.

"Will, it's me. Luke. And Charla and Ian."

Will squinted at the strangers. Should he know these people? They seemed to know him. "Listen, I think I'm lost. I'm looking for a boat called the *Phoenix*. Know it?"

The three exchanged an uneasy glance.

"The *Phoenix* sank, Will," said Luke. "We were all on it."

"What are you talking about?" Will stormed. "I've never been on a boat in my life! Where's Lyssa?"

"She didn't make it," Charla said gently. "The four of us managed to get on the raft, but we never found Lyssa or J.J."

"I don't know any J.J.! I don't know *you*! Where's my sister?"

"Will, think!" urged Luke. "You have to remember! We were all together on the CNC trip. There was a storm and then an explosion. We're lucky to be alive!"

"Listen," Will said impatiently, "you've got the wrong guy. *My* boat trip hasn't started yet. I don't know anything about any shipwreck!"

Charla tried reason. "Please, Will. Try to remember! We were shipwrecked together. How else could we get to this island?"

"You mean Guam?" Will was exasperated. "I *flew* here! With my sister!"

"This isn't Guam," Luke said soberly. "We don't know where we are."

"That's *your* problem!" He looked past them into the gloom. "Lyssa! *Lyssa!*"

"It must be amnesia," Ian said in a low voice.

"You're crazy!" exclaimed Will.

"No, really," Charla pleaded. "You were so sick on the raft! You were unconscious for days — "

"That's a lie! What have you done with my sister?"

Luke stepped forward and put a comforting hand on Will's shoulder.

Wild with panic, Will shook him off and staggered back.

"Will, don't!" Charla cried. "We can help you!"

Like a hunted animal, Will stared from face to face. They were lying, all three of them. They were trying to trick him into — what?

He had no way of knowing. He was lost — so lost. But whatever was going on, these three were mixed up in it somehow. He was in trouble, and who knew what had happened to Lyssa!

Animal instinct took over. With an inarticulate cry, he wheeled on the sand and sprinted down the beach.

He stole a quick glance over his shoulder.

They were gaining on him! The girl ran like a cheetah. "Leave me alone!" he yelled. Desperately he made a right turn and disappeared into the jungle. Charla was hot on his heels.

"No!" cried Ian. "If we get lost in there, we won't even find one another!"

Charla stopped just inside the trees. "We can't just leave him!"

"We can't help him if we're worse off than he is," Luke argued. "We've got to stay cool."

"But — " She began to cry. "It starts bad and just gets worse and worse! Losing the captain was terrible enough. I keep seeing it in my sleep. Then Lyssa and J.J. And now Will — "

"We haven't lost him," soothed Luke. "Maybe the bugs will drive him out of there. They did it to us."

"And maybe they won't!" she sobbed. "He could trip and break a leg. He could fall unconscious again. There are wild boars out there!"

"They're not hunters," Ian put in. "The Discovery Channel did a show on them once. They can be nasty, but they won't hunt a fellow animal for food."

Charla was bitter. "Will's not an animal; he's our friend."

"In the jungle, we're all animals," Ian said seriously. "We have to hunt and forage to survive."

Luke eased himself down on the soft sand. "A wild pig means only one thing to me," he said, rubbing his stomach. "Bacon."

Charla sat beside him. "We can't even open a coconut. You expect to track a boar, kill it, skin it, and cook it? We don't even have a fire."

"That should be job one," Ian said positively. "A big bonfire would signal ships and planes that we're here. Then we could get Will to a doctor."

Charla looked out into the great blackness of the sea. "Do you *really* think we have a chance of being rescued from this place?"

Luke considered the problem. "The whole CNC thing is about isolation. They start you in Guam, which is nowhere, and they take you out to nowhere squared. And this" — he gazed around the beach — "this has to be even farther than that."

"But they'll definitely look for us," Ian argued. "I mean, they send in half the army when some balloonist or mountain climber gets lost. They'll search for us when we don't show up back in Guam."

"Searching and finding are two different things," Luke pointed out. "In case you haven't noticed, it's a really big ocean with thousands of islands that look exactly like this one. Who knows how long it could take to track us down?"

"Months," Charla predicted mournfully. "Years. Never, maybe."

Her words seemed to hang there for a long time, underscored by the steady pounding of the ocean.

It was Ian who finally broke the gloomy silence. "It's not impossible, you know. There are thousands of stories of survival in places like this."

"Maybe so," Luke said grimly. "But I'll bet there were even more that didn't get told because the people were never rescued. Remember, the Discovery Channel can't interview you when you've vanished off the face of the earth."

CHAPTER FOUR

Day 2, 11:55 A.M.

A single ray of tropical sunlight caught the left half of Ian Sikorsky's glasses. Carefully, the boy angled the lens to reflect the intensified beam onto the pile of leaves on the sand in front of him.

There was a breathless silence. Then —

"It's not burning," Charla observed, worried.

"The leaves are still a little damp." Ian's eyes never wavered from the tiny dot of light concentrated on the brush.

"No, they aren't," she said. "We've been drying them out on the beach for three hours."

"You've seen how it rains here. They're wet." A tiny but clear note of exasperation — Ian had little patience for people who disputed what was obvious.

There was an almost inaudible sizzle, and a tiny curl of smoke rose from the pile. And then — a newborn flame.

Charla let out a sigh of relief and realized she'd been holding her breath.

Luke was hard at work using vines to tie together a framework of branches for a lean-to shelter. He ran over to help Charla and Ian arrange kindling in a pyramid around the pile of burning leaves. Soon the fire was going strong. Larger and thicker pieces were added and the flames grew.

"How big does it have to be?" asked Charla.

"Big enough to be spotted from a distance at night," replied Ian.

"It'll be harder to see during the day," Luke pointed out.

"True," agreed Ian. "But if we notice a plane or boat, we can pile on wet leaves. That'll make a lot of smoke."

Wood gathering was a problem. Since they had no cutting tools, their fire had to be fueled by fallen branches and other deadwood. Stumps and thick logs were rare. Thinner twigs were plentiful, but they burned quickly. That meant a huge amount of wood had to be stockpiled to keep the fire going.

The three castaways made dozens of trips into the jungle that afternoon, returning with armload after armload of wood. It was backbreaking work. The sun was searingly hot, and the crushing humidity weighed them down as if they were wearing hundred-pound packs on their backs.

Luke was amazed they were able to do it all. Just yesterday, they had washed up on this island, more dead than alive. It showed what a long drink of water and some solid food could do.

In that area, things were improving. Just down the beach, a single spike of coral stuck out of the sand. Charla gave it its name: the can opener. Coconuts, tough, round, and stubborn, broke like eggs when smashed against it. That morning, she had shown why she was one of the country's top young athletes. She had shinnied up a thirty-foot palm tree as easily as she strolled the beach. From there, she sent a dozen coconuts plummeting to her friends on the ground. After durians, coconut meat seemed as delicious and substantial as a twelve-course meal. The sweet milk tasted better than any triple-chocolate shake Luke could remember.

They had also discovered banana trees. Finger bananas, Charla called them, because they were small — about as long as an index finger. They were light and sweet and plentiful. It was starting to look like starvation would be the least of their worries.

But that was only because they had a lot of worries, Luke reminded himself. Will . . .

He shook his head to clear it. Will was probably okay. They had to look after their own survival first. Then they could search for Will.

By midafternoon, the shelter was complete.

The three were as proud as if they had just built a skyscraper. It definitely wasn't beautiful, but it was a very functional structure. The framework of branches and vines was propped and tied against two trees at the edge of the jungle. Into it, they had tightly woven palm fronds to create an angled roof.

"It won't keep out the rain," Luke had said to Ian, who was the lean-to's designer.

"We'll put pieces of tree bark on top," Ian decided. "If you pile them thick enough, it's perfect for waterproofing."

Luke grinned at the boy. Ian had been sent on this trip because his parents were worried that he had no friends and spent all his time watching TV and surfing the Internet. But now, those hundreds of hours in front of the Learning Channel and *National Geographic Explorer* were starting to pay off. Without Ian's know-how, Luke reflected, they would all probably be dead.

Luke and Charla took the raft that had carried them to the island and propped it against one open end of their new home. The opposite side, which was going to serve as the entrance, they draped with a large, slightly charred piece of sail from the *Phoenix*. This had been saved by Ian from the burning boat and used as sun protection on the raft.

That left just the back end — the space between the two trees. There, Luke and Charla placed another framework of branches, with palm fronds basket-woven through the twigs.

"It's not exactly the Hilton," Luke said with a shrug, "but it'll keep us dry. The sand should be comfortable for sleeping."

They had been working nonstop since the sunrise had awoken them ten hours earlier. Now the castaways allowed themselves a thirty-second period of relaxation.

They were exhausted from their labors, and still weary from their ordeal on the raft, but when their eyes locked, there was perfect understanding and agreement among the three.

"Let's go get him," said Ian as they headed into the woods to search for Will.

CHAPTER FIVE

Day 2, 4:40 P.M.

At that moment, the three might not have recognized Will even if they'd found him. In a single night, their friend had changed. His face had been bruised by branches and scratched by the sharp edges of palm fronds during his frantic escape in the pitch-black. He couldn't believe how thick the foliage was here. At one point he had stumbled into a stand of ferns so dense that he'd been thrown back as if the plants themselves had pushed him away.

What was left of his body after that went to the mosquitoes — clouds of them, coming in waves like the Air Force on a bombing run. He'd tried slapping them away at first. But there were far too many — and too much of his skin left uncovered. Eventually, hundreds of bite-bumps grew together into a horrible shell of puffy red mottled skin. His face felt expanded, deformed. His eyelids were swollen partway shut. The discomfort was unbelievable — far more than itch. His entire body crawled with a churning irritation that scratching only made worse.

Sleep? — Hah! Who could sleep in a state

like that? Curled into a miserable ball on the ground, roots digging into his side, ants parading over him, mosquitoes . . .

Ugh, mosquitoes.

He had broken down during the night, screaming, *"How could you do this to me?!"* At that moment, he didn't care who heard him or even what happened to him. It was all so useless! He didn't even know who he was yelling at.

His parents? They had sent their son and daughter halfway around the world for a boat trip, but this couldn't have been their fault. Lyssa? She was rotten, sure, but not rotten enough to do *this*. Probably she was a victim just like he was.

Those kids? Luke, Charla, and that little guy — Ian?

Will peered out from behind a leafy fern and watched them disappear into the jungle, calling for him.

How did they know his name?

They had to be in on it somehow. They talked about Charting a New Course. And Lyssa . . .

Of course they could have gotten Lyssa's name from him. If only he could think straight!

It must be the mosquitoes. . . .

He stepped out onto the beach. A tiny droplet of blood hit the sand, and he quickly buried it with his tattered sneaker. He didn't want them to know he was watching them. He'd woken up with a leech clamped onto his cheek. It didn't hurt much — he barely noticed it, in fact, over all that itch. But the bite wouldn't stop bleeding.

The *creatures* they had here in Guam! Leeches, bugs, lizards, some kind of hairy wild pigs.

Frowning, he squinted at the crude shelter and the bonfire roaring beside it. If those kids were in on this, why were they living like cave people?

The shipwreck story, of course. Their whole lie was that the *Phoenix* had sunk, and they were marooned here. So they had to act like castaways. Only — why bother playing the game in the first place? Will was alone, stranded, defenseless. What threat did he pose to them?

His head pounded as he struggled to reason it out. Even though it was daylight, he still saw everything through the same silver-gray mist. But there wasn't a cloud in the sky! Maybe it was sun glare acting on eyes that were little more than slits.

A fresh blast of fear stiffened his body. They were after him! It was the only explanation. They needed him for something, and they couldn't leave until they had him.

Well, they won't get me!

He took a few steps back toward the jungle and froze.

This campsite was primitive, but it had fire, which was a lot more than he could say for his own sleeping arrangements. Although this was a hot climate, last night had been damp and chilly.

He rummaged through the woodpile and came up with a sturdy twig, which he held to the flame. In a moment he was wielding a torch. Tonight he would have his own fire.

His swollen eyes fell on the cabin top propped against the side of the shelter. He read the letters: N-I-X.

N-i-x . . . *Phoenix*?

He had a sudden fleeting vision of a tall ship. A schooner — two masts, her white sails gleaming in the sun as she glided through the harbor.

No, impossible. He mustn't let himself be duped.

He examined the sheet covering the entrance to the structure. It was canvas, with brown charring around one edge.

His fevered mind traveled back to Luke's words from the night before: *There was a storm and then an explosion. . . .*

An explosion.

"No," he said aloud. "You're trying to trick me. . . ."

He was about to bolt, to run for the trees, when he saw it. Just inside the shelter — two big bunches of finger bananas.

Food.

He set his torch down in the fire and attacked the meal with a ferocity that alarmed him. It was over in minutes, and he was still hungry, almost as if eating had unleashed his full appetite. And now dozens of peels lay on the sand, evidence of his presence there. He could get rid of them, but that wouldn't explain what happened to all those bananas. . . .

He stood up, mind racing. He couldn't let those kids know he was spying on them. He retrieved his torch and held it to the shelter. The dry twigs and bark went up like a tinderbox.

There, that should destroy the evidence. Except for footprints. And Will's looked no different than the hundreds made by those three kids. No way would they be able to tell they'd had a visitor. They'd have to blame the fire on the wind.

By the time he'd reached the trees, the entire lean-to was engulfed in flames.

CHAPTER SIX

Day 3, 9:05 A.M.

Stupid, thought Charla.

Stupid, stupid, stupid!

She dropped her armload of twigs for their new shelter. *Stupid to put the old one so close to the fire.* "What a waste of time," she complained.

Luke appeared, hauling a thin log that would be one of the main posts. "We're marooned on a deserted island," he reminded her. "Time is the one thing we've got lots of."

"Big joke," she muttered.

He awarded her an encouraging slap on the shoulder. "We were dumb. We'll know better next time. We won't put the lean-to where the wind can blow the fire into it."

She winced at the memory. By the time they'd returned from looking for Will, there had been nothing left but a pile of ash. Only their raft had been spared — the second blaze the cabin top had survived, although it was badly burned. The half name, *NIX*, was barely visible under the brown scorching.

"Come on," said Luke. "We need more vines."

In the jungle, they found Ian snapping branches off a large tree that had fallen over. "Jackpot," he called. "I'll bet there are enough sticks to fill in the whole roof and front."

Soon a huge pile of twigs sat on the soft ground beside them. Charla gathered up as many as she could carry and started back for the beach.

Suddenly, a long thin shape dropped from a treetop. It landed on Charla's shoulders and quickly wrapped itself around her neck.

Ian made the identification. *"Snake!"*

Charla tried to wrench it away, but the harder she pulled, the tighter the long body coiled around her.

"Yeow!" Needlelike teeth sunk into the skin just above her wrist.

Ian picked up a rock and smacked the snake on its squarish head. Dazed, it loosened its grip, and Luke managed to yank it off Charla.

"Get rid of it!" she commanded.

Luke threw. The snake was whirled away in a whiplike motion. It hit the ground and recovered with lightning quickness, lifting itself nearly vertical.

"Look at that muscle control," breathed Ian. "It's balanced on no more than a few inches of its tail."

"You know about these things?" Luke panted.

Ian threw his rock, missing the snake by inches. In a flash, it darted up a palm trunk and disappeared. "It's a brown tree snake," he explained. "We have to be more careful. There are zillions of them on Pacific islands like this."

"Never mind that," snapped Charla, holding her bleeding wrist. "Is it poisonous?"

The younger boy shook his head. "But you don't want the bite to get infected. You should soak it in salt water in the ocean."

"Good idea," agreed Luke. He turned to Charla. "Take a swim. We'll carry this stuff to the beach."

With long, powerful strokes, Charla cut through the waves. Her wounded wrist stung a little from the salt, but she was fine. Better than fine. She was amazed at how quickly her training had asserted itself. She could almost see the Olympic-sized pool at the Y. Breaststroke, butterfly, backstroke, freestyle — how many lengths had she done in that thing? A thousand? Ten thousand? At least. All of them timed by her father and his ever-present stopwatch.

She tried to judge her present pace, deducting time for wave motion and current. A breaker caught her in the face and brought her back to reality. Was she crazy? What did it matter if this swim took three seconds or three hours? She was shipwrecked in a primitive wilderness. She might never again see civilization, much less any swim team. Only a fanatic would continue training *now*.

Abruptly, she stopped swimming and stood on the sandy bottom. She *was* a fanatic when it came to training. That was how she'd gotten herself booked on the *Phoenix* in the first place.

On shore she could see Luke and Ian hauling armloads of wood out of the jungle. She felt a twinge of guilt. She should be helping instead of practicing for an event that was never going to take place. The sooner they were finished, the sooner they could continue their search for poor Will.

Bright flashes of silver caught her eye, and she looked down into the waist-deep water. A school of footlong fish darted all around her. She experienced a moment of fear — were they piranhas?

She relaxed. Whatever they were, they seemed just curious, investigating a novel shape in their ocean.

The next thought to flash through her mind was: food. Her years of training had made a healthy eater of her. She'd always said that she could survive happily on nothing but fruit. But after only a couple of days, if she saw another banana or coconut, she was going to scream.

Could she catch a fish with her bare hands? Were these things even edible? Ian would probably know, but by the time she could ask him, the school would be long gone.

It was a cruel reality out here in nature, yet in a way it was very fair. No judges to appeal to, no instant replay. You make a mistake and your boat sinks, or your shelter burns down. If she was going to do this, she had to do it *now*, without thinking.

A lightning thrust. She stabbed at the water and came up with a wriggling silver body.

Thunderstruck and delighted by her catch, she uttered a piercing shriek and began wading ashore, juggling the fish. Startled by her scream, Luke and Ian raced across the sand to her side.

"What's the matter?" barked Luke.

"Lunch!" she crowed. "I caught lunch!"

"It's a small bonito," put in Ian. They looked blank so he added, "Very edible."

Lunch thrashed wildly.

"But it's not dead!" Luke protested.

"Well, make it dead!" she insisted.

Obediently, Luke reached out and slapped the fish over the head with his open hand. The bonito went on struggling.

"Here!" Ian held out a short stick, part of their construction material.

Luke grabbed it and took a swing just as Charla, shocked, pulled back her hands.

Whap!

"Ow!"

Lunch dropped to the wet sand. Before they could react, the bonito flipped its way into an oncoming wave and disappeared into the surf.

"You were supposed to hit the fish, not me!" Charla snapped.

"You moved!" Luke accused.

They stared at each other for a moment and then burst out laughing. Relieved, Ian joined in. As their merriment died down, they heard another sound. Not the usual island noises — insects and birds and the lapping of the waves. This was mechanical — the drone of motor and propellers.

Ian was the first to look up. *"A plane!"*

It appeared as a dot in the sky that grew bigger and better defined. It was a twin-engine seaplane. And there was no doubt about it — it was heading for their little island.

"They must have seen our fire!" cried Charla, excitement vibrating her thin frame.

Ian frowned. "You know, the chances that we were spotted within a day because of a small bonfire are a million to one. I don't understand how it could have happened."

Luke slapped him on the back. "It happened because we got lucky for a change!" he said, choking back tears of emotion. "We've got to find Will! Now we can get him to a doctor."

They ran along the shore, waving their arms and cheering.

The plane roared right over their heads and started across the island, its pontoons barely clearing the tops of the trees.

"Hey, where are they going?" cried Charla.

The aircraft disappeared over the jungle. The castaways waited for it to circle back for them, but it never did. Instead, they heard the engine power cut back, indicating descent. A few minutes later, the noise of the motor disappeared altogether.

Luke was dumbfounded. "Why would they land all the way over there?"

"They didn't see us," breathed Charla, devastated.

Ian thought it over. "Maybe they're not here

for us. Maybe there's a village or outpost on the other side of the island."

"It's still good news," Luke decided. "We just have to get over there and ask them to give us a ride somewhere. Even if there's no room for us, at least we can get them to send help."

"What if we can't find them?" asked Charla.

Luke started out along the beach. "That plane landed in the water. If we follow the shore, we'll hit it sooner or later. Let's not waste any time."

Charla hurried after him.

"Wait," called Ian. He picked up the stick and wrote WE'RE ALIVE in the hard flat sand by the water's edge.

"Just in case they come looking for us while we're gone," he explained, rushing to catch up with the others.

What started out as a walk along the beach soon got a lot harder. Just around the bend from their campsite, the sandy shoreline ended, giving way to coral outcroppings and steep cliffs. In places, the rocks were so jagged and unclimbable that the three were forced to venture inland to make it over the rough spots.

"Keep your eyes on the water," Luke ordered when they had to veer through a dense grove of trees. "We don't want to walk right by that plane."

"How far do you think we've come?" asked Charla, swatting mosquitoes.

Ian looked thoughtful. "It's hard to say. We make great time on the beach, but when we have to start climbing, we're doing more up and down than forward. Three — maybe four miles."

It was like an obstacle course. Much of the coastline was a series of coves shaped like giant bites out of the shore. These had to be followed around, or sometimes waded through. High rocks bound the inlets, so the castaways were constantly climbing. As they rose with the terrain, their hopes rose with them — only to be dashed when they reached the top. For there lay another identical cove. The view was breathtaking, spectacular. But they had rescue on their minds. Any view that didn't include the plane was a bitter disappointment.

"I hope they haven't left already," said Charla. "We've been at this for three hours."

"We would have heard the engine," Luke panted, starting down into another inlet.

The next rise was a steep one, becoming a sheer cliff near the top. Luckily, there was a grove of leafy saplings on the crest. Luke was able to hoist Charla high enough to get an arm around one of the narrow trunks. With her gymnastics training, she pulled herself to the top. Then, locking her ankles around the base of the tree, she hung herself downward. This allowed the others to use her as a human ladder. They climbed up her athletic body to the flat area at the summit.

"Look!" breathed Ian, pointing.

It was the seaplane — not in the next cove, but in the one after that. It bobbed gently in a shallow lagoon formed by the curve of the coastline and a high jetty of dead coral. Four men waded in the waist-deep water, unloading crates from the cargo hold.

For nine days, the castaways had seen no living soul other than one another. Now — rescuers. With a plane.

Luke's heart was pounding in his ears so loudly that he could barely hear his own voice. "Hey! Over here! Over *here*!"

Charla and Ian began jumping and bellowing.

The four men continued ferrying their cargo. No one looked up.

"We're too far away!" Ian exclaimed, his throat hoarse from shouting.

Charla was in a full panic. "Let's get over there!" She started down the steep slope to the next cove so fast that the others, following her, tripped, fell, and rolled all the way to the beach.

They sprinted along the shore, running the anchor leg of a long race. Down at sea level, they could no longer see the plane and its four occupants. But Luke kept a vivid picture of them in his mind. It gave his feet wings as he started up the incline, right behind Charla. This was it. Beyond this rise lay rescue.

The slope was rocky, but shorter and much less steep than the last one. Charla leaped expertly from foothold to foothold. Luke was hot on her heels. His hands and knees bled from the sharp coral formations, but he didn't care. Nothing mattered — nothing except reaching those men.

He could see the top now, just a few feet away. Charla was already reaching for it . . .

Bang!

The shot echoed six times before Luke stopped counting. His arm snaked out, grabbed Charla by the back of her shirt, and pulled her down beside him. At the same instant, he used his other arm to halt Ian in his tracks.

"What's the matter with you?" Charla shrilled. "We're almost there!"

"That was a gunshot!" Luke hissed.

"No, it wasn't!" she argued. "Maybe the plane backfired or something!"

"Maybe," Luke said doubtfully. "But we've got to find out, one way or the other, before we let them know we're here."

Carefully this time, they crept up to the top and peered over the peak.

There was the seaplane. But now there were only three men wading in the lagoon. And one of them, a tall cadaverous figure with bright red hair, was holding a small snub-nosed revolver.

"Where's the other guy?" Charla whispered urgently.

Then they saw him — floating facedown in the clear water of the lagoon. He wasn't moving.

They ducked back from the top of the hill. Silently, they put together the sights and sounds of the last few minutes and realized that they equaled death.

Charla looked from face to face. "What? You're not saying we're not going down there?"

"We just witnessed a murder!" Luke insisted. "And those guys did it! I don't think they're going to be really psyched to see us!"

"I won't testify against them," Charla promised. "I know that sounds selfish, but we're talking about our lives! *Will's* life!"

"That's exactly why we can't go!" Luke argued. "Look — these are bad people. I don't know what they're doing, or what's in those boxes. But if those guys'll kill one person, they'll have no problem killing us!"

Charla began to shiver. "I'm sorry!" she quavered. "But this is so unfair! There are rescuers right here and we can't even go to them! We'll never see another plane. *Never.*"

"It's unbelievable," agreed Ian, his voice hollow with shock and disappointment. "It would be better if nobody had come at all."

Luke nodded grimly. He turned their dilemma over in his mind every which way, but it always came out the same: They would have to conceal themselves from these men; that was definite. But if he, Charla, and Ian were hiding, how could they ever hope to attract rescuers in a passing plane or boat?

It was the only safe path. But would following it condemn them to a lifetime marooned on this terrible island?

CHAPTER SEVEN

Day 4, 6:20 A.M.

Will Greenfield's "camp" was less than half a mile from his fellow castaways', in a small clearing in some dense jungle. It wasn't much of a clearing, but then again, it wasn't much of a camp. A small fire was the only comfort. Will slept on the cool ground, wedged between tree trunks. A hump created by exposed roots provided his pillow.

Not exactly a four-poster bed, Will reflected, but he didn't seem to need much sleep anymore. Crazy but true — his bug bites and the on-and-off rain kept him awake; his fear and racing mind kept him alert. He lay down because, in the pitch-dark, there was nowhere he could go without getting lost. Even then, he only dozed off here and there. Mostly, he squinted at the fallen log that stretched over him, suspended a few inches above his chest. In the dim firelight, he could see thousands of ants scurrying across the rotting deadwood. A metropolis of them! They made him even more restless. They all seemed so *busy*. Watching them marching to and fro filled him with an urgent desire to *do* something.

The fire helped. Last night he had spent hours using a jagged rock to sharpen straight sticks into arrows. At least it had felt like hours; there was no way to judge time when the sun was down. And at very first predawn light, he was off through the jungle in search of a piece of wood he could use as a bow.

A bow and arrow. Even now, it seemed nuts. Like he'd ever have the guts to shoot at someone!

The idea sobered him up. Those kids were dangerous. He still wasn't sure how, but they'd gotten him separated from his sister, lost on Guam. They were keeping him from the *Phoenix*, which might have left without him. His life could be in danger; Lyssa's too. They were after him, and he was outnumbered, three to one. He needed some kind of weapon to defend himself.

He began testing twigs for their flexibility. The first snapped in his hands, and he dropped it with a yelp of shock. He was a wimp, that was for sure. He'd never even been in a fistfight, except with Lyssa. That was another story. He and Lyssa could really mix it up. No joke. They'd even put each other in the hospital once, which was why they'd been sent on Charting a New Course.

Even though Lyssa was a first-class pain in the butt, he would have given anything to see her face right now. Lyssa was smart. She'd be able to figure out what was going on. Every time he tried to think it through, the mist came back, and with it the terrible headaches.

Aw, Lyss, you're never here when I need you!

He found a supple green branch that was gnarled into a C-shape. Perfect.

He began experimenting with vines. Most broke at the slightest tension. Those that held up were too stiff. At last he found one with both strength and springiness. Carefully, he plucked off the leaves and knotted the ends to his bow.

Now to test it.

He positioned an arrow against the vine and drew it back. Even though no one was watching, he felt himself reddening. Who did he think he was, Robin Hood? He could almost hear Lyssa taunting him:

If you shoot anything besides yourself with that . . .

Before he could finish her sentence, there was a violent rustling, and out of the underbrush burst a dark blur.

Will froze in terror. It was one of those wild pigs! No, bigger than that — a boar! It had to be. The thing was a beast, with black fur and a swinelike appearance. It ran at full speed, no holds barred. Will was sent flying as the animal charged at him. Dark blood appeared on the calf of his leg where a sharp tusk had brushed by.

By the time he could scramble back up, the animal was bearing down on him again. Luckily, the boar was as disorganized as it was ferocious. It thundered every which way, turning constantly. Yet each charge was made with the utmost purpose. Gasping and snorting with rage, it wheeled for another assault.

A tree! Will thought desperately. *Climb a tree!*

In a panic, he looked around. Plenty of trees, but all the close ones were palms — long, smooth trunks, difficult to climb. His eyes fell on the bow, which lay on the ground right where he'd dropped it to make his escape. Where was the arrow?

Then he saw it, partly hidden by a fern. It stuck straight up, its point buried in the soft earth.

In an instant, his mind ran through all the reasons this was a bad idea: *You'll never make it in time. You haven't tested it yet. You'll put your eye out. Look at those tusks. . . .*

He dove just as the boar sprang forward. He picked up the bow and rolled, flailing an arm for the arrow. When he felt the stick in his palm, he yanked it out of the ground, sat up, aimed, and let fly.

The arrow shot from its bow at a wild angle, just as the attacking animal leaped. It caught the boar in the side of the snout, right behind its flat nose. Direct hit!

Wham! Will crumpled back to the ground as the animal's full weight slammed into him. It was on top of him. He could see it, feel it, smell it. He waited for the ripping force of the tusks to tear into him.

And suddenly, the black fur that filled his field of vision was gone. The wounded boar reared up like a frightened horse, squealing in pain. Then it turned tail and disappeared into the jungle once more.

Will lay flat, the bow across his stomach, waiting for the beating of his heart to return to normal. When his brain finally unfroze from terror mode, it was to admit a single thought:

I need more arrows. Lots more.

CHAPTER EIGHT

Day 4, 6:55 A.M.

Ian Sikorsky crawled out of the rebuilt shelter, scratching at ant bites and squinting through the brilliant morning at the lean-to's roof.

Rain had come on and off all last night. Huge clammy droplets had fallen like bombs from the shelter's ceiling. The three castaways had barely slept a wink. According to the documentary he'd seen, tree bark was supposed to be waterproof. It was a lesson he'd been learning over and over again since the sinking of the *Phoenix*: Real life wasn't the same as TV.

He sighed miserably. If he'd come to that conclusion a month ago, Mom and Dad probably never would have sent him on Charting a New Course in the first place.

The thought of his parents, so far away, choked him up a little. Odd, the things he missed the most. The labeled diagram of the solar system that hung on his wall — he couldn't remember the names of two of Saturn's moons. His goldfish, Dot and Com. Even his mother's pot roast, which was practically lethal, and the sound of his father practicing his trombone . . .

He forced himself to concentrate on the problem at hand. Did the roof need more bark? Different bark? Bigger pieces laid out in a new pattern? Mud for mortar, maybe?

Luke would know. He always knew what to do. It wasn't that he had so much information — he just knew exactly how to use the information he had. Ian could memorize the encyclopedia and still not be able to come to the courageous decisions that Luke made every day.

If there was one good thing to come out of this horrible situation, it was getting to know a great guy like Luke Haggerty.

The rain began again. At least the Discovery Channel had been right about that. The tropics were wet in the summer.

Look on the bright side, he told himself. Rain meant drinking water.

The castaways still hadn't found a freshwater stream or spring on the island. There probably wasn't one — they were rare on small cays like this. That meant they would have to survive on what fell out of the sky.

He walked over to the spot on the beach where they had stuck twenty-eight coconut shells in the sand to serve as rain-catchers. Along with them was a yellow rubber rain hat, which Ian had rescued from the burning *Phoenix*. Full marks to TV for that. The hat had been their only source of water on the raft.

"Aw — "

Each shell held maybe a couple of inches of water — less in the hat, which was wider. It was another example of how TV and reality were two different things. Yes, setting out receptacles would gather rain. But not *much* rain. The storms here were heavy but quick. For a good supply of water they'd need a lot more shells — or Noah's flood. With a sad shrug, he picked up the rain hat and drained it. Then he downed three coconut shells in rapid succession. It wasn't enough — not nearly enough. But this was all they had, and he wouldn't dream of drinking more than his share.

When he finished, he was even thirstier than before. It was a different kind of thirst than they had experienced during those awful days on the raft. That had been a burning, paralyzing feeling of parched desperation — you knew that if you didn't drink, you'd be dead very soon. Here there was always *some* water — a pint when they needed a quart; a quart when they needed a gallon. Enough to save their lives, but not to satisfy their constant craving. This was a kind of thirst that could go on for weeks, months, maybe even years. It wouldn't kill them, but it was sure to do something even scarier. It would wear them down and drive them mad.

Angrily, Ian took one of the empty shells and hurled it with all his might. It hit the sand and rolled, disappearing over the shelf where the beach angled down toward the water.

The guilty feeling came immediately. Who was he to throw away one of their precious rain-catchers? He ran over to retrieve it.

And froze.

His heart pounded like a drum solo in his chest. The effort to keep from passing out claimed every ounce of strength he had.

A body lay limp and motionless in the sand. Its lifeless outstretched arms framed a single word from his sign partially erased by the tide: ALIVE. Another bad joke in the long cruel comedy routine that had delivered them all here.

He couldn't bring himself to move any closer. If this was J.J. or Lyssa —

No, it was a grown man. The captain . . . ?

"Luke! *Luke!*"

The sound of his own voice, thin and high-pitched, terrified him. It must have terrified the others too, because they came running. All three fixed their eyes on the huddled shape and moved slowly toward it as though wading through molasses.

It was Luke who mustered the courage to reach down and roll the body over. Pasty gray skin and wild staring eyes. The face looked unreal, like a wax figure.

A collective moaning sigh escaped them. This was not the body of Captain Cascadden.

"It's the guy," gasped Luke. "The fourth man from the plane." He pointed to a neat bullet hole, dead center in the victim's forehead. "We were right. They killed him."

"But that happened all the way on the other side of the island," Charla said weakly. "What's he doing here?"

"The current must swing around this way," Ian decided.

He couldn't take his eyes from the fatal wound. Whatever blood had been there had been washed clean by the hours in the ocean. Now the bullet hole was exactly that, a hole — an empty space.

In the past two weeks, they had all come to know death. Captain Cascadden of the *Phoenix* had been swept overboard. Their shipmates Lyssa and J.J. had been lost at sea. They had all seen Will descend into unconsciousness, and then a fevered amnesia that could cost him his life. But this was the first time any of the castaways had ever been face-to-face with a real dead body.

It was stunning, gut-wrenching, horrifying, yet oddly mesmerizing. None of them could take their eyes away. But it also presented an awkward problem.

Charla was the first to bring it up. "Uh — what are we going to *do* with him?"

"We can't just leave him there," Ian put in. "His body will decompose. And birds and animals will . . ." His voice trailed off. When would he ever learn to shut up? No one wanted to hear it!

"We'll give him a decent burial," Luke said suddenly. "I know people who never got funerals no matter how much they deserved them. We've got the chance to bury one guy. Let's take it."

As soon as the words were out of Luke's mouth, Ian knew it was the right choice.

He was full of admiration. *That's what it takes*, he guessed, *to be a leader*.

In his own mind, Luke wasn't so sure. Burying a fully grown man was going to be a huge job — especially without shovels or any kind of digging equipment. They were probably still weak from the raft. They had eaten nothing but fruit in over a week; they were getting water, but not much. Yes, this was the right thing to do. But did it make sense?

No one wanted to touch the body any more than absolutely necessary. They rolled the dead man over onto the blackened cabin top and carried it like a stretcher into the jungle.

"Let's take it *far* in," Charla suggested.

Luke understood instantly and agreed. This man could not hurt them now. But a grave was a reminder of death. If they buried him in the nearby woods where they foraged for food and firewood, they would be inviting death into their daily lives.

The body was heavy, the going rough. Some groves of trees were so dense that the raft wouldn't fit between the trunks, so they were forced to change direction. On they trudged. They kept going mostly because they didn't know where to stop. They were kids on a boat trip. How could they have been ready for all that had happened? Shipwrecked. Adrift at sea. Marooned. And now this.

Crazy, Luke thought. The guy was dead. He wasn't exactly going to be enjoying the view. What difference did it make where they buried him?

He stopped. "Right here," he decided.

Then came the digging. They had no tools, so they used their bare hands. A crisscrossing lattice of thick vines had to be torn away. It was filthy work. The three were soon covered in dirt, which mixed with dripping sweat to form a layer of slimy mud. Was this how Will was living in the middle of the jungle? Bugs everywhere. Worms the size of garter snakes, huge winged cockroaches, giant slugs, strange fat caterpillars — bagworms, Ian called them.

Was it crazy to think that Will was alive somewhere in this never-ending wilderness? They hadn't seen so much as a trace of him in three whole days. Maybe his memory had come back and he was trying to find them, but he was lost in the vast sameness of the jungle. There were so many ways to get hurt out here. An unseen vine, a bad fall or broken ankle — he'd be at the mercy of the snakes; no way to get food or water . . .

Don't think. Dig.

The hole took over an hour. Finally, they lifted the body off the raft, dropped it inside the grave, and filled in the dirt. For Luke, even the burning and sinking of the *Phoenix* had been easier to stomach than this terrible task.

The others felt it too, an overpowering desire to put this gruesome experience behind them.

"Let's get out of here," Ian panted when the last handful of dirt was in place.

"No," Luke said simply.

"Come on," urged Charla. "This is creepy. We buried the guy; let's beat it."

"Not yet," Luke insisted. "Somebody should say something."

"We don't even know his name," she complained.

"He's probably got a driver's license or passport or something like that," Ian put in. "We never checked."

Charla was impatient. "You want to go digging for it?"

"Let's just get it over with," said Luke. He had only been to one funeral in his life — his great-uncle's. His parents had gotten him all decked out in his best suit. He looked around. He and his fellow castaways were clothed in ragged shorts and T-shirts, ripped, faded, salt-encrusted, and filthy with mud. Their sneakers were battered and full of holes. They weren't exactly dressed to deliver a eulogy.

Not knowing what to do, Luke stood at attention, as if they were playing the national anthem at a ball game. Ian put a hand on his heart.

"For all we know, you were a bad guy and you got exactly what you deserved," Luke began. "But maybe somebody somewhere is going to miss you the way our families miss us. They won't know where you are, or why you don't come home, or what's happened to you. And that's got to feel pretty sad."

A muffled sob escaped Ian. Charla put an arm around his shoulders.

"Or maybe that person misses you the way we miss Lyssa and J.J., who never got any funeral, not even a lame one like this. Or maybe it's more like Will — we know he's out here, but — "

His voice broke. All three of them were crying now. Even at the times of greatest desperation on the raft, they had never wept like this. The sun was high in the sky — more than half the day, wasted. . . .

Suddenly, Luke's sorrow transformed itself into a flare of anger. Anger at the judge for sentencing him. Anger at Mr. Radford, the mate of the *Phoenix*, for deserting them. Anger at himself for letting Will get away. Anger even at the man in the ground, for dying and putting them through this.

The moment passed. He drew a deep breath. "Anyway, what do you care?" he finished to the mound of earth at their feet. "You're already dead."

"Amen," Ian barely whispered.

"Rest in peace," added Charla.

The ocean, thought Luke. That was the only

way to cleanse them of this horror. A good long swim. He bent down to pick up the raft.

"Wait!" Ian exclaimed suddenly.

The younger boy was pointing at a small gap in the underbrush not ten feet from the grave site. Right there in the soft ground — footprints.

Will.

CHAPTER NINE

Day 4, 2:40 P.M.

"He's alive!" Luke exclaimed with relief. He cupped his hands to his mouth. "Will! *Will!*"

Charla grabbed his arm. "Not so loud," she warned. "There are killers on this island!"

"That's another reason we have to find him," Luke retorted. "Before *they* do!"

They listened breathlessly. Birdsong. Chirping of insects.

"Come on, Will," called Luke, a little lower this time. "We know you're out here."

Nothing.

And then, barely audible amid the sounds of the jungle . . . a far-off human voice.

"It's coming from over there!" chorused the three castaways.

They regarded one another in dismay. They were pointing in three different directions.

Luke checked the sneaker print. It was heading to their left. "This way!"

He started off, leading the others. It was pure guesswork, Luke thought. Any other footprints were covered by heavy underbrush. In his mind, he kept an image of the direction of Will's sneaker tread and tried to follow it like a compass needle. Not that it was possible to stay on course in this tangle of greenery.

But when you have only one clue, you follow it.

"Please, Will!" Charla tried to make her quiet voice carry.

They trudged on, searching for any sign of human life — a broken branch, a trampled fern, a torn vine. But nothing stood out.

And then Ian found another footprint.

"You're right!" exclaimed Charla. "Two of them!" She stared. "Uh-oh."

"What's wrong?" asked Luke.

"If this is Will," she said slowly, "he's got two different-sized feet."

Ian knelt. "And two different shoes." He looked up at Luke. "This is two people."

Luke drew in his breath sharply. "Are you sure?"

Charla began to tremble. "The men from the plane!" she breathed. "It's not Will, it's them!"

Ian frowned. "But what are they doing all the way over here?"

"I don't care if they're on an Easter egg hunt," put in Luke. "We've got to get out of here before they come back!"

And then . . . just the tiniest *crack*.

They froze and listened. It was the swishing and snapping of people walking through the jungle.

Luke mouthed the words, *Get down*, and the three dropped, trying to disappear into the dense underbrush.

The swishing was louder now. The men were close! Luke tried to catch a glimpse of them, but he didn't dare move for fear of being spotted. Where were they? Since there was no trail, it was impossible to predict what path someone might take.

Suddenly . . . a flash of red shirt! Luke's breath caught in his throat. Just a few feet away! *The killers were walking straight at them!*

It was too late to run. Luke rolled to his right in a desperate attempt to avoid the stepping foot. Horrified, he felt the sneaker catch him on the shoulder.

"Hey!" came a voice above him.

A split second later, the figure was tumbling into the underbrush behind him. The jig was up. They were caught.

Luke didn't think; he just reacted. In a single motion, he grabbed a rock and jumped upright, aiming at the back of the intruder's blond head. "One move and you're dead!" he hissed.

Ian picked up the sunglasses that had fallen off the prisoner as he tripped. They were strangely familiar — sleek and silver, designer frames. He flashed Luke the earpiece. On it was engraved: JONATHAN LANE, THE TOAST OF LONDON — P.S.

Luke's eyes bulged. These glasses belonged to J.J. Lane, their shipmate from the *Phoenix*! There was no mistaking them! They were one-of-a-kind — originally given to J.J.'s father, movie star Jonathan Lane, by Paul Smith, the fashion designer!

Luke dropped his rock. "J.J.?" he barely whispered.

The actor's son rolled over. *"Luke?"*

"You're alive!" cried Charla, throwing herself at J.J. in a joyous embrace. Ian piled on. Luke was slapping backs, shoulders — any surface he could get a hand on.

All at once, he stopped celebrating and grabbed J.J. by the shirt. "Lyssa — ?"

"Relax — "

And then a familiar voice said, "Do you think these are, like, you know, real bananas?" Lyssa Greenfield stepped into view, a bunch of finger bananas in her arms. She gaped at the four of them rolling around the underbrush. Dumbstruck, she grappled for words. "But you're dead!" she gasped finally.

"*You're* dead," Luke shot back, laughing with relief.

"Man, what happened to you guys?" asked J.J. "You look like coal miners."

It took Lyssa a few seconds to do a head count and realize who was missing. "Where's my brother?"

"Don't panic," Charla said quickly. "He's not dead — at least he wasn't three days ago."

"Why isn't he with you?" she demanded, her voice shrill.

"He ran away from us," Luke explained. "He doesn't remember us; he doesn't remember the trip — he thinks he's lost on Guam and it's all our fault."

She was shocked. "He's gone crazy?"

"Amnesia," Ian supplied.

"He's lost his memory?"

"Just the last couple of weeks of it," Luke replied. "He remembers *you* — he kept asking us, 'What have you done with my sister?' Almost like we kidnapped you or something. He thinks the *Phoenix* is moored at a marina around here, and he has to get you and report for Charting a New Course."

"I saw a show about it once," added Ian. "It's called paranoid delusion."

"We've got to find him," Lyssa said urgently. "I can make him remember."

Charla put a reassuring arm on her shoulder. "We'll keep looking. But it's hard to find someone who doesn't want to be found."

Lyssa blinked back tears. "But you haven't seen him for three days! He could be dead!"

"Or he could be just avoiding us," Luke pointed out. "That would be good news — it means he's alive and alert."

"Can he really survive all by himself on this island?" she asked dubiously.

Luke spread his arms wide. "Can we? He has what we have — which is pretty much nothing."

"Except the supplies on the lifeboat," put in J.J.

"Lifeboat?" Charla repeated.

"The inflatable raft," J.J. explained. "That's how we got away when the boat sank. It's still in the little cove where we washed ashore. We've been living in it."

"How did you guys get here?" asked Lyssa.

"On a piece of cabin top the size of a postage stamp," Charla explained. "One of us had to hang over the side or we'd capsize. You were lucky."

"Hey," the actor's son interrupted sharply, "I could be in L.A. right now, surrounded by fast cars, hot tubs, and chicks, chicks, chicks. Don't lecture me on how I haven't suffered enough."

"No fighting," ordered Luke. "We're all in this together, right? We're scared, we're worried about Will — and we're all sick of coconuts and bananas."

J.J. and Lyssa looked completely blank.

"Maybe you've been eating durians," put in Ian.

"They're hungry, not crazy," Charla mumbled distastefully.

"We've been eating what's in the boat," said Lyssa. "You know, the freeze-dried survival meals. Chicken and mashed potatoes. Beef stew. Chili."

Luke looked so genuinely ravenous that even Lyssa had to laugh. "Put your tongue back in your head. We've only got one left — mac and cheese. That's why we're out in the jungle — looking for food."

"I love mac and cheese," piped up Ian. His face fell. "But I guess we should save it for a special occasion."

J.J. stared at him. "Special occasion? We're in the middle of nowhere! Remember how nowhere we were on the boat? Well, that was the Sunset Strip compared to here! What special occasions are we going to have? National Cockroach-the-Size-of-a-Volkswagen Day?"

Luke was thoughtful. "How about Raft Moving Day? The lifeboat is too easy to spot out on a beach. We should move it to the cover of the trees."

"But being spotted is the whole point," argued Lyssa. "How are we going to get rescued if nobody can see us?"

Solemnly, Luke filled in the newcomers about the murder they'd witnessed and the body that had washed up on the beach.

"It's a real jam," he finished. "If rescuers don't find us, we'll die here. But if we make ourselves visible enough to get rescued, these guys will spot us first, and *they'll* kill us."

"Will," Lyssa said nervously. "They'd kill him too. And he probably doesn't even know they're out there."

J.J. spoke up. "Doesn't anybody else think this is kind of fishy? The boat sinks; we're stranded; murderers on the island — I mean, whose luck is this bad?"

"It even happens to rich people," Charla told him resentfully.

"It's fake," J.J. scoffed. "I say we're still on Charting a New Course, and all this has happened to us on purpose. The boat sank because it was *supposed* to sink — you know, a trick boat. The special effects guys who work on my dad's movies, they could rig something like that in a heartbeat."

Everybody groaned. This had been J.J.'s theory from the beginning.

"The whole point of the trip is to make us forget what a bunch of losers we are and force us to work as a team," he went on. "Well, it's happening. These so-called criminals, they could be actors hired by CNC. They're just another test for us. And we're falling for it — man, we're performing like a bunch of trained seals!"

"You're disgusting, J.J. Lane!" Lyssa snapped at him. "My poor brother could be dying this minute — "

"That's even more evidence that I'm right," J.J. interrupted. "Will got a little too messed up so they stepped in and scooped him out of the game. He's probably watching us on hidden camera right now, eating a steak and laughing his butt off."

"That was a real murder we saw," Luke said darkly. "And it was *definitely* a real dead body."

J.J. shrugged. "When my dad was doing this horror flick, he once brought home a fake disembodied hand from the prop room. It looked so real that my stepmom — number three — she practically had a heart attack."

"You know, it almost doesn't matter," Ian said thoughtfully. "Whether it's a setup or not, we're still shipwrecked and we have to survive."

"Except CNC won't let us die," J.J. reminded him.

"There are exactly two reasons why we're not dead," said Luke grimly. "Dumb luck and coconuts. And the luck ran out when that plane landed. It doesn't get any scarier than this."

CHAPTER TEN

Day 4, 5:25 P.M.

Voices.

Will reacted immediately. He snatched up his bow and a handful of arrows.

He could hear the swish and crackle of legs making their way through heavy underbrush.

They were coming to get him.

And they were close.

He made a move to put out the campfire and froze. That fire was the only thing that kept the bugs away at night. His mosquito-bite bodysuit was finally starting to recede; the churning itch had become almost bearable. He could even open his eyes all the way now, although the silvery mist was still there, and the headaches were worse than ever. How could he willingly feed himself to squadrons of hungry insects?

There must be some way . . .

He jammed the arrows in his back pocket and slung the bow over his shoulder. Then he picked up a sturdy twig and held it to the fire.

The voices were getting louder. From the babble, he made out a single word: *Phoenix*.

They were talking about the boat!

His new torch blazing in his hand, he stomped out the fire and kicked a mass of vines and dead leaves to cover the evidence. Then he squeezed himself into a dense stand of ferns and peered out.

It was the little kid — the one who called himself Ian. His companion was a tall blond boy Will hadn't seen before. The newcomer was laughing.

"I swim to the life raft and climb inside, and then it hits me: I forgot to untie the line! The boat's sinking, and *I'm still attached to it*. So I'm hanging over the side trying to chew through that rope with my teeth — which isn't easy because *it's on fire*."

Will frowned. More lies about the shipwreck. But why tell them to each other?

He froze. Did they suspect he was listening? That made no sense. They'd come get him if they knew where he was. Why were they talking about a disaster that never happened?

"Wasn't there a knife in the survival kit?" Ian was asking.

"Yeah, but who's got time to look for it?" the older boy exclaimed. "I'm chewing for my life here! Then, the *Phoenix* starts down, and I'm thinking, 'That's it. I'm dead,' " and, poof, the rope burns through, and I'm free! These CNC guys — when they scare you, they don't mess around."

"It seems pretty far-fetched that they could be behind all this," said Ian.

"You'll see. We're wasting our time. Will's not on the island anymore. He's probably in some hotel room, living large."

Hotel room? What was he talking about?

As Will watched the blond boy, in a flash he knew with absolute certainty something he couldn't possibly have known. It was a message engraved on one of the earpieces of the kid's sunglasses: THE TOAST OF LONDON.

The toast of London?

He was taken aback. Where would he get a crazy idea like that? This was a total stranger! And yet the feeling was so vivid Will could almost see the words imprinted in the fancy metal.

Impossible. And yet it wouldn't be the weirdest thing that had happened to him in the last few days.

Was he losing his mind?

And then he heard a word that had been very much in his thoughts lately: Lyssa.

"Yeah, she was already in the water when I found her," the blonde was saying. "I'm not sure how she got there. We'll ask her."

Ask her! Will stiffened like a pointer. They knew where she was!

He struggled to force his sluggish mind to reason it out. He couldn't let them get away. He had to attack! There were two of them, but he had his bow and arrow. He would squeeze his sister's whereabouts out of them if it was the last thing he did. If they wouldn't talk, he'd . . .

What? Shoot them? He'd never have the guts.

He thrummed the bowstring with his free hand. *Yes, I would. This is life and death. I shot that boar and I'll shoot them.*

The two boys were no more than twenty feet away. Will prepared himself to spring. They would never get any closer than this. . . .

The moment passed. Will squinted at their receding backs. He took no action.

There was a better way.

CHAPTER ELEVEN

Day 4, 9:45 P.M.

Luke shone the beam of the flashlight at the survival pack.

Just that simple act seemed like a miracle. Only yesterday, the setting of the sun had signified the end of all activity on the island. Darkness was final, total. Now they had artificial light, courtesy of the inflatable raft.

While J.J. and Ian had searched for Will, Luke and the girls had moved the covered lifeboat from the small cove where it was beached to a spot just inside the trees at the castaways' camp. It wasn't easy to maneuver such a bulky object through heavy jungle — it had to be rolled, carried, squeezed, and sometimes tossed. But it was all worth it when Luke took the cover off the survival pack.

"We're rich," he breathed.

No, this was much better than money.

Conveniences.

Small aluminum pots, pans, plates. Plastic cups and cutlery. Compass. Knife. Lighter and waterproof matches. First aid kit. Fishing line and hooks . . .

There it was. Macaroni and cheese. A hole opened up in his stomach. Fruit could keep them from starving, but this was *real* food. Big too. The label read: SERVES TEN.

He had an insane desire to bite into the package — straight through the shrink-wrap. Ha! The others would kill him, and they'd be right. He set it back in the survival kit. This was their last meal, their safety net. They had to preserve it for when they were really desperate.

He hefted the raft's water keg. It was almost empty, but it would still come in handy. In the coconut shells, the rainwater was always mostly evaporated by the time they got around to drinking it. Now they had a reservoir they could close. That was a big help.

To keep us alive so we can die here, he thought suddenly. *Or be murdered.*

That was an ongoing battle — Luke's brain versus his morale. He got through the days by setting realistic goals for himself: Find food. Find water. Keep looking for Will.

Two shipmates you'd written off as dead showed up today, he reminded himself. *If that won't keep your spirits up, nothing will.*

He sighed. These days, survival included winning these arguments with himself.

With the keg under his arm, he ducked out of

the raft's sun canopy that loosely covered the lifeboat like a tent. The other four sat around the fire. The dancing light of the flames played across their faces. It felt unreal, like a movie scene. Luke guessed that he had interrupted a conversation.

He picked up a coconut shell, careful not to spill a drop. "From now on, let's use this keg to store our water."

"Good idea," said Lyssa. "Hey, Luke, what do you think happened to Radford?"

Luke clenched the shell harder. Out of six crew members who hadn't been too fond of the *Phoenix*'s mate, Luke had the strongest feelings. "Personally, I don't think about him at all," he replied sourly. "But now that you mention it, I hope the biggest shark in the ocean swam up and bit his ugly head off."

Radford had proved to be much more than just a seagoing bully. With the boat crippled and slowly sinking, he had slipped off during the night in the schooner's twelve-foot dinghy, taking most of their food with him. In effect, he had left them to die. It had been that predicament — and their efforts to restart the engine — that had led to the explosion and fire that had scuttled the ship.

"But do you think he could have made it back to Guam?" asked Charla.

"Rat-face is an experienced sailor," Luke mused, emptying another shell, "but he was in the open Pacific in a tiny boat. One good wave could have flipped him."

"He's fine," scoffed J.J. "It's all part of the game."

"In your fantasy world," Charla added unkindly.

"Well, he never could have survived for real on that pile of Popsicle sticks." The actor's son shrugged. "His own B.O. would have killed him."

"Big joke," snorted Luke. "That guy's as bad as the men from the plane. Worse, because he was getting paid to look after us." His wrist shook, and he brought his lips to the coconut shell to suck up the spilled water. "Just hearing his name again makes me nuts."

The five had decided to bed down in the inflatable lifeboat. The sand of the beach was soft and comfortable, but four nights of ant bites had convinced them it was time for a new home. As the others retired to divvy up sleeping space, Lyssa remained outside to trim down their fire — a sensible precaution to avoid being noticed by the men on the other side of the island.

It was an eerie feeling: killers out there, somewhere in the blackness. Almost too much to accept. After everything else that had happened — murderers on the very same tiny cay where both groups of castaways had washed ashore.

She saw a flicker of light coming from the woods. Her first reaction was panic. It was them!

She squinted into the gloom. Nothing. Were her eyes playing tricks on her?

Suddenly, a hand reached out from behind and clamped down hard over her mouth. Her scream was smothered by the powerful grip. She struggled, but her attacker had too firm a hold.

And then — a whisper in her ear:

"Cut it out, Lyss! It's me!"

Will? If he hadn't been clutching her so tightly, she would have dropped like a stone from relief.

You're alive! What happened to you? Don't you remember the shipwreck? The thoughts darted around in her head. There was so much to say. But when she opened her mouth she couldn't speak. Mute, she wheeled and embraced her brother. He resisted for an instant and then wrapped his arms around her. They held each other with an intensity that momentarily canceled out the danger, the horror, the fear. A small part of Lyssa, standing strangely distant from herself, noted that this was the first time she could ever remember hugging Will.

She found her voice at last. "I can't believe it's you."

"Shhh!" He stiffened, pulled back. "They'll hear us. We've got to get out of here right now!"

"Will, they're our friends."

"Don't listen to them, Lyss," Will warned. "Everything they say is a lie. They told me you were dead."

"They thought I was," Lyssa reasoned. "I thought the same thing about them after the boat sank. About you too."

Clutching his torch, Will backed up a step, wide-eyed with shock. "They've got you brainwashed!"

"No — "

She stopped herself from arguing, because, for the first time, she had gotten a really good look at her brother. He had lost weight — they all had, but it was much more noticeable on the sturdy Will. His hair was matted, his eyes wild, and he had more bug bites than skin. A crude bow was slung over one bony shoulder. He smelled terrible. He was like a savage, she thought in agony. She had no hope of reasoning with him. In fact, she could think of only one way to save him.

"Luke!" she cried. "Everybody! Come quick!"

Shocked by the betrayal, Will turned to run. She lunged at him, wrapping her arms around his thin frame. He shook her off roughly. Her foot hooked on a low vine, and she fell heavily to the ground.

He turned to face her. "I'll be back, Lyss — I promise! I won't let them do this to you!"

By the time Luke and the others burst out of the lifeboat, he had fled into the jungle, the flicker of his torch disappearing in the density of the trees.

CHAPTER TWELVE

Day 4, 11:10 P.M.

The jungle was becoming familiar to Will. Who would have dreamed that he would ever know one clump of ferns from another?

But he did. No, that wasn't exactly true. The individual plants all looked alike, especially by torchlight. It was the progression that he was beginning to recognize: coconut palms on the right, broad-leaf whatchamacallits on the left, big step over the fallen log, those weird crisscrossing ferns dead ahead — he was almost home.

He felt a twinge of pride. He used to be the kind of kid who fell apart when the cable went down, or when the family ran out of microwave popcorn. An eight-minute power failure threw him into a panic. But now he was making his way through dense jungle on his own, in the near-blackness of night.

If only Lyssa could see him.

She *had* seen him, he reminded himself. Barely ten minutes ago. And she had refused to come with him. How was he ever going to rescue her?

To rescue Lyssa, he thought, *first you have to rescue yourself.*

But how would he accomplish that? Where should he go? What should he do?

For a moment, the silvery fog swirled around him once more. He closed his eyes and fought through it. And when he opened them again, he was at the twin palms of his camp.

He brushed a few handfuls of dried leaves onto the remains of his fire and reached down with his torch.

The kindling caught quickly, and in the glow of the sudden flare, he saw that he was not alone.

At first, the creature looked like a small haystack. Then the massive head swung around and whimpered.

Will jumped. It was the wild boar.

Run for it!

He stood poised, waiting for the attack. It didn't come.

The animal whimpered again.

Will squinted in the firelight. Blood stained the bristly snout where the arrow still protruded.

His hand tightened on the bow over his shoulder and he pulled an arrow from his pocket. He could kill this thing. Kill it and eat it.

Yeah, right. You're too squeamish to dig out a splinter.

He took a step forward.

Careful. Nothing's more dangerous than a wounded animal.

But this one was dying.

Well, duh! That's why you shot it, right?

Cautiously, Will approached the boar and squatted down beside it. The red piggy eyes seemed almost colorless now, sunken into the head/snout/body. He leaned over until he was close enough to feel the hot wind of the boar's tortured breathing. The animal regarded him suspiciously, but made no attempt to move. He reached out a hand, and the boar shrank from him, but it lacked the strength to get up.

When he closed his hand on the shaft of the arrow, the boar squealed in pain, shaking its snout. Luckily, the arrow pulled out smoothly and easily — there was no barbed head, just a sharpened point at the end. Fresh blood trickled from the hole.

Why was he doing this? This animal was protein, and easy hunting too. Protein meant energy, and energy was what he needed to rescue Lyssa and figure a way out of this mess.

Will fitted an arrow into the bow and pulled back, straining to aim for the creature's neck.

What neck? It's all neck! Its butt is practically an extension of its neck!

He circled the boar, aiming behind its ears. It regarded him through distant, colorless eyes.

Will was sweating now. This Guam humidity always made him perspire, but now it was pouring off him like Niagara Falls. Why couldn't he do this? It was so stupid. He ate bacon cheeseburgers all the time. This was no different.

Except, Will thought, *when you go to McDonald's, you can't feel your dinner's hot breath on your leg before you eat it.*

He set down the bow. "Tell you what," he said out loud to the boar. "I'm going to find some more wood for the fire. You've got till I get back to beat it."

But when he returned with an armload of twigs, the boar hadn't moved an inch.

"I'm going to take a little nap. If you're not gone by the time I wake up, you're dinner."

Sleep would not come. He kept peeking through half-closed eyelids at the boar, which was still in its spot by the fire.

"Will you get lost?!" raged Will. "Don't you realize your *life* is on the line?"

But somewhere, deep down, he had a sneaking suspicion that the boar was smarter than he was.

Will glared at the animal. "You don't think I've got the guts to do it! Well, you're wrong! You've got the rest of the night to scram. If you're still here at sunup, I'm having boar cutlets for lunch."

In the morning, he awoke to find his legs numb and tingling. He looked down the length of his body. The boar was fast asleep, curled up on his feet.

"Aw, come on, boar, get off!" He kicked himself free, struggled upright, and limped around, trying to restore his circulation. The boar followed him like an adoring puppy.

"You're supposed to be *gone*." Will was half disgusted and half pleased.

The boar rubbed against Will's legs, knocking him over with its sheer size and weight.

"Hey, cut it out, boar! Boar?" Down he went, landing flat on his behind. "I guess I'd better give you a name," he laughed. "I can't just call you *boar*."

But what did you call a hairy, squinty-eyed slob with no neck and a bad attitude?

"I know." He grinned. "Pig-face."

A frown. Pig-face fit to a T, but another name came to mind — Rat-face.

That made no sense. The face was piggy, not ratty.

Why did the name sound so right? And so familiar?

"Rat-face," he said out loud.

The boar spit out a mouthful of chewed leaves and delivered a resounding belch.

And Rat-face it remained.

CHAPTER THIRTEEN

Day 5, 8:05 A.M.

In addition to much-needed shelter and supplies, the inflatable lifeboat provided an unexpected bonus with its sun canopy: darkness. For the first time since they had landed on the island, the tropical sun didn't wake up Luke at dawn.

He would have slept hours longer — they all might have — if it hadn't been for the noise. It was distant at first, but it grew louder and louder. The castaways listened intently. It was the buzz of an airplane engine. Could that mean — ?

"Are they leaving?" Ian asked excitedly.

"Please, God," breathed Charla.

They scrambled out of the raft and looked up for the twin-engine seaplane. But the dense canopy of branches and palm fronds blocked out the sky except for tiny glimpses of bright blue here and there.

"The beach!" exclaimed J.J., breaking into a run.

Luke grabbed his wrist and held on. "It's too dangerous! They might see you."

They waited for the slow fade in the engine sounds that would indicate the aircraft was far away. Instead, the buzz remained at full volume, almost as if it were coming from directly overhead. And then, all at once, the noise died out.

Luke frowned. "That's weird."

"You think they're still here?" asked Lyssa.

Charla was confused. "But why would they use their plane if they weren't leaving?"

Ian shrugged. "Maybe they're gone. Sound over water can do some funny things."

"We've got to go over there and find out," Luke decided.

"That lagoon is on the other side of the island," Charla reminded him. "It takes half the day to get there."

"Maybe not," Ian put in. "We've got a compass now. We can estimate the direction and take a shortcut through the jungle. That should save a lot of time."

They retrieved the compass, and Ian lined up the needle with north. "I'd say just about due east," he guessed. "Maybe a few degrees to the south." He rummaged through the survival pack, coming up with the knife.

J.J. was highly amused. "They've got guns, kid. What are you going to do with that? Floss?"

Ian took the blade and made a small cut in the bark of a coconut palm. "I saw a documentary on Lewis and Clark on the History Channel," he explained. "Always mark your trail so you can find your way back."

It was much easier going through the jungle, although they were constantly sidestepping dense thickets, some of them thirty or forty feet wide. In less than an hour, they had reached a low bluff overlooking the shore. There they made a left turn and headed south.

"Hey!"

All at once, Lyssa pitched forward, landing flat on her face in the underbrush.

"Must have been those big island joker ants," snickered J.J., helping her up. "Watch out, they also give wedgies."

"Very fun — " She fell silent in midword, staring at the ground. "I know this sounds crazy, but was there ever a *sidewalk* here, do you think?"

"Oh, sure," J.J. said sarcastically. "They laid it down back when they built the mini-mall — "

"Look!" she interrupted.

Half buried in the damp earth was a familiar gray shape. It was broken and crumbling, with weeds and brush coming up through the cracks. But the edge that stuck out of the ground was perfectly straight.

There was no question about it. This was a slab of poured concrete.

"Here's another," called Charla, kicking at the mud a few feet ahead of them.

They spread out, digging with their hands and feet. They found slabs extending all the way from the bluff, hundreds of yards into the deepest jungle.

"Maybe it's the Walk of Fame," suggested J.J., "where all the celebrity lizards make impressions of their tails in the cement."

"It proves one thing," said Luke. "The island wasn't always deserted. People lived here."

"And later than the invention of paved roads," Ian pointed out.

Charla nodded. "But who builds a road in the middle of the jungle?"

They all turned to Ian, but for once he had no answer.

The castaways continued south. It wasn't long before they spotted the sheltered lagoon where they had witnessed the murder just two days before. To Luke it seemed as if a hundred years had passed since then.

"Get down," he ordered.

The five dropped to a crouch, peering out through the trees.

Lyssa hovered over Luke's shoulder. "Can you see anything? Are they gone?"

There, beached side by side, were two seaplanes.

CHAPTER FOURTEEN

Day 5, 9:50 A.M.

Charla was bewildered. "*Another* plane?"

Luke stared in disbelief, but the truth was undeniable. The sound they'd heard hadn't been the departure of the first aircraft, but the arrival of a second.

"They've got company," he commented.

J.J. frowned. "Yeah, but why meet *here*? This island is less than boring. There's nothing but bugs and bananas."

"Privacy," Luke told him. "These guys are criminals. They're probably up to something illegal."

Ian pointed out a place where the jungle advanced down a coral ramp. There was excellent cover in the dense underbrush, plus it was in spying range of the shore, and a good twenty feet above sea level. It would be nearly impossible for the men to spot them there.

It took another few minutes to creep down the steep slope. Luke was in the lead, with the others in line behind him, keeping their heads low. They crouched in the vines, peering out over the lagoon.

The second plane was a single-engine job, smaller than the first one, but with a large cargo hold on its underside.

"Look!" hissed Charla.

It was the red-haired man. Instinctively, Luke's eyes traveled to the thin man's waist, where his gun was jammed into his belt.

"That's the killer," he whispered to Lyssa and J.J. "The guy he's talking to must be from the second plane."

Four others came into view — Red Hair's partners and two newcomers. They were carrying the crates that had been unloaded from the first aircraft. Red Hair pried open the first box and rummaged inside.

"Blankets?" mused Charla in perplexity.

There was something wrapped in them. It was long and gleaming white — taller than the men themselves. It took two of them to hold it up, and the one clutching the foot-thick base was struggling. The thing tapered in a slight curve down to a soft point at the other end.

"Let me guess," put in J.J. "It's the world's largest golf tee."

Ian's mouth formed an O of sudden understanding. "Ivory!"

Lyssa stared at him. "It's *soap*?"

The younger boy shook his head. "The other

kind of ivory. I think that's an elephant tusk. I saw a show about it once. That's why people hunt elephants. For their ivory."

"But that's *wrong*," protested Charla.

"It's also against the law, isn't it?" asked Luke.

"So's murder," J.J. reminded him darkly.

They watched as the men unwrapped three more tusks — one the same size as the first, and a shorter pair about four feet long. They then turned their attention to a second case. It was smaller, but more high-tech, with sealing latches and various knobs and indicator dials. As they opened it, a cloud of vapor rose and dissipated into the tropical humidity.

"I was afraid of that," Ian said seriously.

Inside they could make out dozens of transparent jars.

"What is it?" asked Luke.

"I think those are animal parts," Ian told them, "probably from an endangered species — tiger, most likely."

"Parts?" Lyssa asked weakly.

"Fur, claws," Ian replied, "meat, vital organs, bones — "

"Yuck," was J.J.'s opinion.

Charla looked as if she were about to throw up. "But why? Who wants that stuff?"

"In a lot of Asian cities, tiger parts are a delicacy for the super-rich, or even a miracle cure. It was all in the documentary I saw. A full-grown tiger can be worth close to a quarter of a million dollars on the streets of Taipei or Hong Kong."

"So what you're saying," Luke began, "is that these guys are smugglers?"

Ian nodded. "Dealers in ivory and illegal animal parts. The men from the first plane — they must buy from poachers around Africa and Asia. Then they sell to the second group."

"But why here?" asked Lyssa.

"Isn't it obvious?" replied Luke. "We're totally isolated. In a million years, the police would never catch them making the exchange."

"It's probably a halfway point too," Ian guessed. "They could be coming from Japan, Korea, the Philippines, Hong Kong, anywhere — even Hawaii."

"That could be why they killed that guy," added Charla solemnly. "Maybe he was ripping them off or something."

They watched grimly as the smugglers went over the rest of the shipment. In addition to three more refrigerated containers, there was an entire crate of what appeared to be rhinoceros horns.

"It's possible that no animals were killed for

those," Ian mused. "You can cut a rhino's horn off and it will grow back. It's actually a type of hair. Then it's ground up and sold as medicine."

By this time, Charla was shaking with outrage. "They probably killed those poor rhinos anyway — just for the fun of it!"

Satisfied that the shipment was in order, one of the newcomers went over and stepped inside the single-engine plane. A moment later, he reappeared, helping an enormously fat man dressed in an all-white silk suit that gleamed even brighter than the ivory.

"Mr. Big," snickered J.J.

"Yes," Ian said seriously. "I mean, that's probably not his name. But he seems to be in charge."

Sweat poured in streaks down the man's face and neck, and he mopped himself with a sopping handkerchief, fighting a losing battle to stay dry. In his free hand, he carried a small suitcase. He was accompanied by the biggest Doberman pinscher Luke had ever seen.

"What's up with the suitcase?" asked J.J. "Is he moving in?"

Then Mr. Big opened the luggage. They goggled.

"Money!" exclaimed Charla in a strangled voice.

The bag was filled with neat bundles of bills,

packed side by side, end to end, and on top of one another. It was a fortune.

Suddenly, the big dog stiffened. Then it began to bark, a loud raspy baritone that cut through the jungle like a hot knife through butter.

"It smells us!" rasped Lyssa, terrified.

"Let's go," whispered Luke.

Charla jumped up. "You don't have to ask *me* twice!"

Luke grabbed her by the shorts and pulled her down again. "*Slowly,*" he insisted. "And stay low till we're well into the woods."

The castaways crawled back up the slope. They could still hear the barking when they reached the top and ran into the depths of the jungle. There was a panic to their flight, and they scrambled through the vines, tripping and stumbling as the foliage grew thicker.

"Slow down!" ordered Luke.

"But what if they come after us?" asked Charla, who was thirty feet ahead of everyone else.

"They probably think he was barking at a lizard or something," said Luke. "Come on, somebody's going to break a leg."

"I'm sorry!" Charla was almost hysterical as she stopped to let the others catch up. "It's just so horrible! Those poor animals!"

"Hey! *Hey!*" J.J. cut her off. "We have no proof that any of that stuff is real. Those tusks could be plastic!"

"So how come you ran too?" she shot back.

"The dog probably isn't in on the hoax." J.J. grinned sheepishly. "Every year hundreds of actors wind up with stitches because stunt animals don't know it's just a movie."

"That's no stunt animal." Luke was angry now. "And this is no stunt!"

"Every time it seems like we've hit bottom, something even more awful happens," Lyssa agreed miserably. "Will goes crazy, or *more* smugglers come, or their dog smells us! How could it be worse?"

She got her answer when they followed Ian's trail back to the inflatable raft. The contents of the survival pack were scattered all around the lifeboat and the surrounding jungle. Precious supplies were opened and strewn every which way.

"Look!" Charla pointed down. There, amid the dozens of sneaker prints, were animal tracks.

Ian squatted to examine them. "Boar," he concluded.

"Uh-oh." Lyssa rummaged through their gear. "Whatever it was, it took the mac and cheese."

"That's impossible!" Luke exploded. "It was freeze-dried and vacuum-packed! It didn't smell any different from the first aid kit. There's no way a pig could be smart enough to go through all this stuff and decide *that* was food!"

His fellow castaways stared uneasily back at him.

Their last meal — their safety net — was gone.

"I don't know which one of us is the bigger pig," mumbled Will, crunching uncooked pasta.

Beside him stood the boar, its snout pumping up and down as the two savaged the freeze-dried macaroni and cheese straight out of the package.

"You know, Rat-face, it's a lot better when you boil it," commented Will to his new companion. He picked up a fistful of orange powder and crammed it in after the macaroni. "The cheese is supposed to be hot and gooey. If I ever get out of here, I'll come back and bring you some."

Rat-face obviously thought it was just fine the way it was. The animal never missed a swallow as it tore at the plastic bag with one sharp tusk.

"Hey, stay on your own side!" snapped Will. "After this, it's back to bananas, you know!"

CHAPTER FIFTEEN

Day 6, 5:35 P.M.

The theft of their last meal changed the castaways' approach to food. No longer could they depend on eleventh-hour runs for coconuts and bananas to stand between them and malnutrition. They needed protein. They needed vegetables. They needed well-balanced meals.

The equipment from the survival pack helped. Suddenly, they had pots and pans. They could fish and cook what they caught. Even durian seeds were tasty when roasted over the fire.

Two forked sticks with a crosspiece allowed a pot to be hung over the flame by its half-hoop handle. This enabled them to boil taro, a native root, which resembled a cross between a yam and an overloaded electrical junction box.

"You know," said J.J. in genuine surprise, "this isn't half bad. It's almost like mashed potatoes."

"It gets very soft when boiled," Ian agreed. "But you have to cook it well to kill off a poisonous chemical that could be fatal to humans."

J.J. spit a mouthful halfway across the beach.

"It's fantastic," beamed Luke, digging in. "The only thing that tastes better than food prepared by your own hands is food prepared by somebody else's."

Taro was plentiful; the fresh water to boil it in was very scarce. While it seemed to be raining constantly, it never rained for very long. No matter how many coconut shells the castaways set out — now over a hundred — the yield was never more than an inch or so.

Ian tried rigging a still — something he had seen on *National Geographic Explorer*. They boiled a pot of seawater under a three-sided plastic tent made from a rain poncho. The water vapor rose as steam, recondensing on the sides of the tent. Then the droplets ran down the inside of the plastic and collected in three bowls on the ground. The salt was left behind in the pot. This was fresh water.

"Seems like a lot of work for a dribble," commented J.J.

"You got a busy social calendar?" laughed Lyssa.

"I could have," sighed the actor's son. "In California."

"That's why you got kicked out of California," Luke butted in. "You were having too much fun."

J.J. glared at him, but had to admit Luke wasn't exaggerating much. His reputation as a wild Hollywood brat had grown almost as large as his famous father's movie career. Gossip columnists used to call to ask about Dad. Now they wanted the details of J.J.'s latest escapade. It had been a great source of satisfaction to him. His brow clouded. Until Jonathan Lane had chosen CNC in the hope that it might straighten out his flaky son.

"How could you do this to me?" he screamed at his father in tortured dreams every night. But the next morning he always awoke knowing that he'd given Dad a lot of help making the decision.

Their social calendars may have been blank, but the castaways had plenty to keep them busy. Two patrols per day — morning and afternoon — were dispatched to comb the jungle for signs of Will or his camp. They all took turns searching, with Lyssa leading the group every time.

Ian built three more stills, so one person had to maintain the fires and keep adding seawater to the pots. This assignment also included emptying the bowls of freshly distilled water into the lifeboat's keg.

Each fishing trip began with a spirited round of rock-paper-scissors to determine who would perform the disgusting task of baiting the hooks. This was a job nobody wanted, because, as Luke put it, "The worms are bigger than the fish."

Charla didn't use bait at all. She preferred the

challenge of swimming in the ocean and snaring her fish with a lightning-quick hand.

J.J. volunteered for fishing every day, but spent very little time with his hook in the water. He had discovered sea cucumbers, and was fascinated and delighted by their life process.

"Picture a bag of guts with a hole at each end," he explained. "The water goes straight through it. But when some poor sap gets beached, it just sits there, full of water. Watch this."

He picked up the creature, aimed it like a water pistol, and squeezed. Instantly, the sea cucumber emptied itself in a thin stream that hit Charla full in the face.

She pushed J.J. into the surf and held him under.

Lyssa hauled him out of the drink. "I guess Charla isn't interested in marine biology," she sympathized.

Ian was in charge of food gathering because he was the only person who could tell what was edible. The good news was that food was everywhere, even on the walls of their home. They would wake up each morning to find the lifeboat covered in giant snails.

"They're a delicacy, you know," Ian told them, gathering an armload, "and a good source of protein."

"In your dreams," said everybody.

But after bananas and coconuts three times a day, most of them were ready to try anything.

When she wasn't in the jungle looking for her brother, Lyssa spent most of her time tinkering with the lifeboat's scorched and broken radio. She was a straight-A student with a real knack for electronics and machinery.

They were surviving, keeping busy, overcoming obstacles. The depression would come suddenly, unexpectedly, without warning. Charla might reach up to smooth her hair, feel the stiff, salt-encrusted tangle, and burst into tears. The crying would sometimes last for hours. Or Ian would grow suddenly silent and sit for half a day, staring morosely out to sea, visualizing who knew what. Any mention of Will could set Lyssa off.

For J.J., it would start innocently enough. He'd be talking about a great pizza place he knew in L.A. But then, forty-five minutes later, he'd be sitting there on the sand, his arms wrapped around himself straitjacket-style, still mumbling about double-cheese and pepperoni.

Charla ate less, exercised more, and blew up at anybody who dared mention it.

"Why don't you just keep on swimming?" J.J.

suggested. "At your pace, you should hit the Oregon Coast in another three years."

"I should hit your ugly face in another three seconds," she retorted.

"Take it easy," soothed Luke.

J.J. turned on him, blue eyes blazing. "Who died and left you God?"

And before Luke knew it, he was shouting, "The captain did, that's who! And if you hadn't decided to run up the sails in a gale, he'd be alive, we'd still have a boat, and none of us would be having this conversation."

Luke watched in angry satisfaction as J.J.'s face drained of all color. It was the one topic J.J. couldn't smirk away. The tears were already on the way when he started running. At the edge of the trees, he turned and spat a single word back at Luke: "*Convict!*"

And then Luke was chasing him, intent on war. But the low vines tripped him up and he landed hard, raging at the sky. "*No!!*"

Wasn't this just perfect? Now — *now*, of all times — everyone was going nuts! Didn't they see that they had to hold it together if they were going to find Will and get off this rock? *Why can't they be more like me?* Luke thought. *I'm calm! Steady! Balanced! Sensible —*

At the sudden pain in his hands, he looked down. His knuckles were skinned and bleeding. With each thought, he had been having a boxing match with a tree trunk.

Sensible and steady. Yeah, right.

J.J. didn't reappear until late that night. He stepped into the lifeboat and tapped Luke on the shoulder. "I'm on fishing tomorrow."

"Okay," Luke replied. "I'll work the stills."

For once, he was grateful there were so many chores.

There was one final task that all the castaways kept up day to day. No matter what other job was in progress, five pairs of ears were always listening for the drone of airplane engines that would mean the smugglers were leaving the island. Until those men were gone, the shipwrecked crew of the *Phoenix* could not light signal fires, or write distress messages in the sand. They would never be rescued if they continued to be forced into hiding.

"When are they going to *scram*?" asked Lyssa in exasperation. "They've got their tusks and their horns. What are they waiting for?"

"That's what we have to find out," Luke said decisively.

So the next morning, Luke and Charla set off for the other side of the island to spy on their unwanted neighbors. Two hours later, they returned, trembling.

"They're searching the jungle!" Charla rasped. "They've got that Doberman sniffing the ground to pick up our scent!"

"You mean they know we're here?" asked Lyssa in horror.

"The dog definitely smells something when it sniffs someplace we've been," Luke told them. "But those guys can't be sure what they're looking for."

"The island's not that big," Ian said nervously. "Sooner or later, I mean, even if it's just by dumb luck — "

He never finished the sentence. He didn't have to. The five castaways stood rooted in the sand as the thought began to sink in.

They were being hunted.

CHAPTER SIXTEEN

Day 9, 10:10 A.M.

They called it the two-minute drill.

The signal came from Charla, atop a palm tree — the hooting of an owl, a sound that would never be heard on a tropical island. That set the vanishing process in motion. The fires were extinguished, the stills folded up and buried in the sand. A few sweeps of a giant fern and their footprints were gone too, leaving a deserted beach.

Two quick kicks took care of the supports for the sun canopy, and the lifeboat lay flat. Ready hands drew a leafy blanket of woven vines and palm fronds over it. Suddenly, the black rubber craft was gone, replaced by the green-brown colors of the jungle. Finally, the castaways themselves disappeared, melting into the dense underbrush.

There was the electronic beep of a digital stopwatch. "One-fifty-seven," Ian reported. "Our best time yet."

Subdued cheering and a few backslaps as the heads popped up again.

Luke wasn't happy. "We can make ourselves

disappear, but we can't hide our smell. The dog's nose won't be fooled."

Ian looked thoughtful. "What if we set out a few fish heads and tails and guts on the beach? That would be a strong enough scent to confuse the dog."

"It'll also gas us out of here," Lyssa noted, making a face.

"We can keep it wrapped up in one of the ponchos," Luke decided. "We'll open it only when we hear the signal."

It was agreed that two-person scout teams would be dispatched to keep an eye on the smugglers. Lyssa objected. This would distract them from the search for Will. But the others overruled her. They hadn't seen Will in five days and had no idea where he was. For all they knew, he was on the other side of the island where the floatplanes were beached. They were as likely to spot him there as anywhere.

"That's another reason to spy on those guys," Luke argued. "To make sure they haven't found Will."

Luke and Ian had been scouting for over an hour before they spotted the Doberman. They immediately pulled back, ducking behind a dense stand of ferns. Red Hair had the dog on a leash, and two other men were with him. All three were armed.

"You were right," whispered Ian. "They're looking for something."

They followed along for a while, making sure that nothing was moving in the direction of the castaways' camp. When the dog began to run in circles, barking excitedly, they knew they had to retreat.

Ian frowned. "Three of them out here. How many are with the planes?"

Luke shrugged. "One way to find out."

They backtracked. Staying low, they eased themselves down the slope to their spying place overlooking the cove. The two boys counted and delivered their tallies at the same time: three — two men on the beach, and Mr. Big sitting half in and half out of the smaller plane. They couldn't see his face, but his thick legs and white suit identified him.

In all this time, not one of the traffickers had changed clothes. Which meant . . .

"They weren't planning to stay here," Luke whispered. "They're only hanging around to make sure there's no one else on the island."

Ian was confused. "Where do they sleep? There's no campsite. And they can't all fit in the planes — not lying down, anyway."

It was a good question. They eyeballed every inch of the cove. There was the lagoon, the rocky jetty, a narrow beach, and coral bluffs leading up to the edge of the jungle. No camp.

"We're missing something," Luke murmured.

And then he saw the footprints in the sand. They were mostly heading in one direction. They ended where the beach did, of course. But Luke could envision the trail leading up the slope and into the jungle. The entry point was perhaps a quarter mile from where he and Ian lay hidden.

There had to be something there — something that was important to these men.

Carefully, silently, they picked their way around the apron of the cove. The jungle became so dense that they were doing more wading than walking. Their progress slowed to almost nothing. That was why Luke didn't injure himself when he bumped straight into it.

"A wall?" Ian gasped.

Three steps before, it had been invisible, knit into the fabric of the rain forest. But here it was, the curved corrugated metal siding of a Quonset hut. A big one.

Luke and Ian stared at each other in mute wonder. Their island — isolated, deserted, and empty of any hint of civilization — had a *building* on it! It was mind-blowing.

Luke put his finger to his lips. Then the two of them crept down the length of the structure. Cautiously, they turned the corner and found themselves facing a gray metal front with a door and two windows. A rusted sign, faded and barely legible, read: UNITED STATES ARMY AIR CORPS.

"An Air Force base?" Luke breathed. "In the middle of a jungle?"

Ian pointed to the sign. "Army Air Corps. They haven't been called that for fifty years. This area could have been clear back then, and the jungle just grew up around it."

Luke sidled up to the streaked and smeared window and peered in. The jungle was growing in there too, blasted up through rotted floor planking. There was no one inside.

"Let's check it out," he whispered.

They opened the door — someone had recently oiled the hinges — and slipped through. Desks, chalkboards, filing cabinets. Yellowed old papers and file folders were scattered everywhere.

"Look!" exclaimed Ian.

Sleeping bags were spread out on the old benches. A few beer bottles, empty food cans, and dozens of cigarette butts littered two desks that had been pushed together. The place smelled of stale smoke.

This was the traffickers' camp, all right. This — what was it? Military, definitely. Old and abandoned, for sure. But a base? It was more like an office.

Ian touched Luke's arm and pointed to a bulletin board suspended from one of the curved walls. Tacked up there was a faded diagram of a hut exactly like the one they were standing in. Two other huts, much smaller, stood behind it. These three buildings seemed to be the extent of this installation.

"Did they have bases this small?" Luke asked.

The younger boy shrugged and drew Luke's attention to something else on the board — a map of the Pacific. Tiny pins representing boats and planes were stuck all over the chart. Fallen ones lay on the floor in front of it.

"World War Two," he noted.

There were a couple of private offices and, farther back, a barracks room with lines of bunks. Luke wondered why the smugglers were sleeping on hard benches when real beds were right here. Then he got a closer look at the mattresses. They were ripped to shreds and alive with thousands of bugs. He shuddered and returned to where Ian was flipping through file folders.

"Find anything?"

Ian shook his head. "Requisitions for toilet paper and shaving cream. They needed a part for their movie projector in 1945 — " He picked up an envelope marked TOP SECRET that had once been closed with an important-looking seal. A dozen or so stapled pages were inside. The first line caught his eye: *Re: Deployment of Junior.*

His eyes widened like saucers. *"Junior!"*

"Junior?" repeated Luke. "Who's Junior?"

The sound they heard next drove every other thought from their minds — the barking of a dog.

They ran for the door. Gruff voices outside. The men were right there! Luke grabbed Ian and spun him around.

The terror was plain in the younger boy's eyes. He mouthed the words, *Back door*?

As they sped to the rear of the building, Luke knew that the answer to that question would mean the difference between life and death.

Heart sinking, he faced the back wall. No door; just two windows. Jammed and warped, the first one wouldn't budge.

The smugglers clattered in the front door, accompanied by their barking dog.

"Shut up, mutt," came an unfriendly growl.

The second window moved only an inch before seizing up against a thick vine.

Ian began to shake.

That was when Luke looked down. The metal

wall of the hut had come away from the decaying floor about eight inches. It was their only chance. Desperately, he shoved Ian into the gap and followed. The two wriggled through to the outside and crawled off into the jungle. There was no running. The foliage was far too thick. But however slow, it felt like escape — desperate movement, propelled by panic. And when the underbrush thinned, they sprinted headlong, tripping and falling, and getting up to run some more.

They were halfway home before Luke managed to get his hands on Ian's shoulders to slow the boy down.

"Ian!" he panted. "What *was* all that back there? Who's Junior?"

Still clutching the top-secret envelope and papers, Ian struggled to catch his breath.

"A bomb," he wheezed finally. "An atomic bomb."

CHAPTER SEVENTEEN

Day 9, 3:40 P.M.

Luke stared at him. "An atomic bomb?"

Ian nodded fervently. "It was all in this documentary on the Manhattan Project, where they invented the first nuclear weapons back in World War Two. They were supposed to build three bombs, code-named Fat Man, Little Boy, and Junior. But the war ended after Fat Man and Little Boy were dropped. So Junior never had to be built." He waved the envelope in Luke's face. "That installation was going to be used to launch Junior, the third atomic bomb."

Luke looked doubtful. "And the Air Force just *forgot* this place?"

"It wasn't a real base," Ian reasoned. "There were only bunks for about twenty or thirty people. All they needed were a couple of planes and someplace to land them."

"The concrete!" Luke exclaimed. "That was their runway, right? And it just got busted up and overgrown after fifty years?"

"Probably," Ian agreed. He looked scared. "You don't think they're going to miss this envelope, do you? The smugglers, I mean? That would tip them off that we're here."

"They don't care about paper," Luke assured him. "Not unless there's money printed on it. But, man, was that a close call, or what?"

"I'm still shaking," Ian admitted.

Soon they spotted Charla in the lookout tree. "What took you guys so long?"

"Don't ask," groaned Luke.

The powwow was held on the beach over bananas and coconut milk.

"You know, this is a really fascinating history lesson," yawned J.J., "but who cares about what happened in some ancient war? Come up with a fully charged cell phone, and you've got my attention."

"Unfortunately," Luke said grimly, "that old war affects us more than we think. Tell them, Ian."

"I've been going through those papers," Ian explained tragically. "As near as I can tell, this installation was so top secret that they picked an island that was never on any maps. So I don't think we should depend on anyone coming to rescue us because — technically — we're nowhere."

Luke could almost hear a slurping sound as the very last ounce of hope was sucked out of the castaways.

They fell into a gloomy silence that was broken only by the steady lapping of the ocean.

Will's stomach yawned wide open, sore and empty.

It was the mac and cheese, he thought miserably. Before that day, he hadn't known how starved he really was. But the mac and cheese — that beautiful, delicious, *terrible* mac and cheese! Bliss for a few hours. And then the payback.

The meal had served only to awaken the monster of his hunger. That's how it seemed to him — a living creature, loose inside him and impossible to control. It had started as a rumbling in his belly and had grown to a roar that was drowning out everything else around him. He had tried gorging himself on bananas — dozens of them. But the sheer quantity had made him sick. And still his hunger raged. No, it was beyond hunger now. It was desperation.

A numbing terror rose from the tips of his toes as the fact of his helplessness became clear. He was becoming weaker every hour. Soon he wouldn't be able to *act*, to rescue Lyssa, or even to save himself. All alone in the jungle, there was only one place this could lead, one way it could end.

He was going to die.

But I'm not all alone. . . .

His fevered gaze fell on the boar, curled up and snoring between the twin palms.

Rat-face is food. Rat-face . . .

He reached for his bow and pulled an arrow back against the string.

But —

Go close. That'll give you a quick kill.

He stopped short. How could he even think of killing Rat-face? The boar had been his only friend these last few days — maybe the final days of Will's whole life.

Food. That was all that mattered. This wasn't about friendship. It was a matter of survival.

He drew back the arrow.

Harder! he exhorted himself. If the first shot reached the brain, there would be no suffering.

His eyes filled up with tears. "I'm sorry, Rat-face," he whispered.

As soon as the name passed his lips, he had a startling image of a burly, sour-looking sailor standing on the deck of a ship. It was so vivid that Will could actually make out the word painted on the man's life jacket: PHOENIX.

Shocked, he relaxed his grip on the bow-string. The arrow snapped off the stretched vine, its dull end hitting him in the eye.

"Ow!"

He staggered a little, but he hardly noticed the pain over what was going on in his head. It all came rushing back with the force of a runaway train — the other kids, the storm, the explosion, the shipwreck! And those terrible days of drifting on the raft, parched and starving, not knowing if his sister, Lyssa, was alive or dead.

He felt a great swell of joy in his chest. She wasn't dead — he had seen her and talked to her. That was real, wasn't it? And the others too. By some miracle, they had all survived the sinking of the *Phoenix* and had drifted to the same place, wherever it was.

The others! He had been hiding from them, calling them liars and kidnappers, stealing their food, vandalizing their camp. And their only purpose had been to help him.

They must think I'm crazy!

He considered this. They were right. He *was* crazy. Or at least he had been.

Not anymore.

"Come on, Rat-face!" he exclaimed excitedly.

The boar awoke and shot him a questioning look.

"Let's go!" He ran off into the jungle, Rat-face trotting along at his heels.

CHAPTER EIGHTEEN

Day 9, 4:05 P.M.

Smell was a problem for those who lived on the island. In this heat and humidity, just the regular chores of day-to-day survival wrung the perspiration out of the five castaways. Someone was always battling jock itch or athlete's foot or a weird tropical fungus. If it hadn't been for their easy access to the ocean, the stink of the whole group would have been unbearable.

It was always harder to notice on yourself. Luke risked a sniff when nobody was looking. Pee-yew! The mud of his and Ian's tunnel out of the hut and the sweat of their desperate escape had mingled with the usual jungle steaminess to create a pretty strong funk.

Bathing was always a tricky tightrope to walk. With the girls around, Luke wanted his privacy. But he didn't want to be like Ian. The kid was so shy that he would go miles up the beach, and a simple bath would end up taking him all day.

He walked along the shore, past the can opener, to where the sand gave way to rocky coral. He kicked off his shoes and dove through the incoming breakers, letting his clothes wash on his body. He was no expert swimmer like Charla, but he enjoyed the ocean. This was the only good thing about being shipwrecked, he reflected. No beach at home had such perfect water, clear as glass, with not the slightest trace of the murkiness of pollution.

He pulled off his shirt and swished it through the waves like a washing machine agitator. Then he wrung it and spread it on the rocks to dry. Next he wriggled out of his shorts and underwear and did the same. Then he went for a long swim. The water felt cool and refreshing, and some of the tension loosened in his neck and shoulders. Even though it was deep here, he could clearly see plants and rocks and starfish on the bottom ten feet below.

Peace. The ocean was the only place he ever found it, where he could free his mind from the terrible danger all around him. He didn't forget his problems here. But he could somehow separate himself from them. There were times where he could even remember the old Luke Haggerty, the one from way back before this avalanche of troubles had started with that lousy locker inspection.

Here he could lose himself in the pounding of the surf, the screeching of gulls, the rustling of the wind through palm fronds, the hooting of an owl. . . .

An *owl*?

The signal!

Luke must have swum, but he didn't remember a second of it. The next thing he knew, he was scrambling onto the coral, cutting his feet, shins, and knees to ribbons as he leaped into his shorts. Then he was pounding up the beach. He could see his fellow castaways performing their two-minute drill. The wind roared in his ears as he sprinted — that and a different, terrifying sound: the approaching bark of a hunting dog.

He arrived at the scene at the same time as Charla.

"Two men!" she hissed, pushing sand over a dismantled still. "And the Doberman!"

Luke was proud of the group. There was panic in their eyes, but their bodies were pure efficiency. The stills disappeared beneath the beach. Their footprints were wiped clean. Then into the woods, where they flattened the lifeboat and pulled the palm blanket on top of it.

By now, men's voices could be heard along with the barking. The castaways melted into the underbrush.

"What's the deal with this dog? It's going crazy!"

They were no more than a hundred feet away.

Crouched next to Luke, Charla froze in shock

and horror. "The fish!" she breathed. "We forgot to open the stinky fish! The dog smells *us*!"

Too late, thought Luke. What he heard next turned the blood in his veins to ice.

"It's onto something!" the other man said excitedly. "Let go of the leash!"

A split second later, Luke caught sight of the brown-and-black Doberman bounding through the underbrush, fangs bared. It was fifty feet away, then thirty. Beside him, he heard Charla gasp. His mind worked furiously. What could they do? He came up blank. For the first time, the castaways had truly arrived at zero options. Their adventure was ending right here, right now.

At that moment, a guided missile shot out of the bushes and slammed full-force into the dog.

It all happened so fast that, for a second, Luke had no idea what was going on. He only knew that, instead of being savaged by a vicious animal, he was still in hiding, watching a monumental struggle.

Then he heard the squeal.

"The wild boar!" he whispered.

The fight was furious and deadly. The boar's head pumped up and down like a pile driver as it slashed at the dog with its tusks. The Doberman lunged and growled, biting at the enemy's throat with razor-sharp fangs. The boar was bigger and much heavier, but the Doberman was faster and more agile, leaping up to tear at the thick neck. The boar's head weaved back and forth, slashing at the dog's exposed underbelly.

Blood began to spatter, but it was impossible to tell which animal it was coming from.

Terrible howling. And suddenly, the dog was on the bottom, and the boar was in charge.

All at once, the two men came crashing through the underbrush. Red Hair was in the lead. "What the — ?" He raised his pistol and fired a shot into the boar's neck.

With a squeal that was half rage, half surprise, the boar pulled back from the Doberman and raised its massive, blood-streaked head.

The second man pulled his weapon too, and he and Red Hair opened fire. It was a scene straight out of a gangster movie — shot after shot, bullets flying. Luke tried to burrow himself into the soft ground.

The boar advanced one menacing step and then became seemingly boneless, collapsing in a heap among the vines, dead.

The two men ran up to where the lifeless Doberman lay.

"I can't believe it!" Red Hair was furious. "That fat tub of lard is gonna blow its blubber over this dog!"

"And all for nothing," his partner agreed in disgust. "It was smelling that ugly hog all along."

"That's the good news," Red Hair commented. "At least now we can leave this godforsaken bug farm." As the two started back through the jungle, he reached out one heavy boot and kicked the dead boar. "Stupid pig!"

Luke's mind was reeling, but he forced himself to remain perfectly still. All would be lost if one of them jumped up too soon before the smugglers were well out of range. It was only ten minutes, but it felt like two lifetimes. There was a rustling of foliage, and Lyssa crept out of hiding and stood over the body of the boar.

"It saved our lives."

One by one, other castaways emerged from the underbrush.

"But why would it fight for us?" asked Charla.

"Maybe he just didn't like Dobermans," Luke suggested. "I know I don't."

J.J. looked into the boar's open, unseeing eyes. "We'll call it even on the mac and cheese, okay?"

Charla clouted him on the shoulder.

"Well, it's just a *pig*," he defended himself.

All at once, they heard a whimper.

Everybody froze. Luke put his finger to his lips.

There it was again. A weak sigh. Barely a breath.

Definitely human.

They looked around. Where could it be coming from? The two men were gone. The castaways were all accounted for.

And then Ian tripped on something. He gawked. "Luke!"

There, beneath a low fern, lay Will Greenfield, white and still. Ian felt for a pulse. It was strong and steady.

"Oh, my God!" Lyssa dropped to one knee beside her brother. The tattered cuff of Will's shorts was soaked red. She pulled the fabric up. Beneath it was a bullet wound, just above the thigh.

"Aw, Will!" she said, voice shaking. "Why is it always you?"

His eyes fluttered open. "Don't yell at me," he said faintly. "I didn't do it on purpose." He waved. "Hi, Luke. Ian. Charla. J.J. Long time no see."

"You *know* us?" blurted Charla.

Will was sheepish. "I do now. Did you guys see Rat-face?"

"Rat-face?" repeated Luke in disbelief.

"Not *that* Rat-face," Will explained. "I've got a pet boar."

Lyssa put a hand on his arm. "No, you don't," she said gently. "Not anymore. But it was a real hero, Will. You can be proud of it."

"Oh." Will looked sad. Suddenly, he winced in pain, grabbing at his wounded leg. "Man, that hurts!" he groaned. "How bad is it?"

Instinctively, they all turned to Ian.

The younger boy backed off. "How should I know?" He added, "But there's no exit wound, so the bullet must be still in there. He needs a doctor."

"They don't make jungle calls," J.J. reminded him. "I'll get the first aid kit."

"Hang in there," Lyssa encouraged her brother. "You're going to be just fine."

She was grateful that he couldn't see how little she believed her own words.

CHAPTER NINETEEN

Day 10, 11:35 A.M.

The stills were up again, their small fires burning, not on the beach, but just inside the trees. In their midst lay Will, stretched out on the small piece of cabin top that had miraculously delivered four of the castaways from a burning, sinking ship to the safety of the island.

"Hey, Lyss, I never said thanks for blowing up the boat."

"*You* were the one who was supposed to be ventilating the engine room," his sister retorted. "Shut up and rest."

It was a pointless argument. But somehow it felt comforting to be bickering again.

She checked the bandage on his wounded leg, not having the slightest idea what she was looking for. "Uh-huh," she said — competently, she hoped.

She joined Ian, who was picking heavy seeds out of a durian and setting them aside for roasting. "The ocean has to be out of fish before I eat those things," she commented sourly.

Ian looked grave. "We've got to get your brother off this island."

"Will's just a big complainer," she pointed out. "That shows he's getting better. The bleeding has finally stopped."

The boy shook his head seriously. "There's going to be an infection for sure with that bullet in there. It's no big deal if you can get medical attention. But our first aid stuff is going to run out fast."

Lyssa blinked. "He could *die*?"

He shrugged helplessly. "Not tomorrow, not next week. But if we can't get him to a hospital — "

"Lyss," called Will from the raft, "could you get me some water?"

"You've got legs!" she snapped automatically.

It was so instant, so instinctive for her to take a shot at him — the result of twelve years of sibling warfare. Practically every detail of her life existed to be in opposition to something about Will. He struggled in school, so she slaved for straight A's. He was cautious, so she tried to be impulsive.

What would she do without him? In a bizarre way, they were a team. They were even named as a pair, after flowers — Sweet William and Sweet Alyssum. A cheesy move by their parents, she'd always thought. But now it seemed wiser and more telling than Lyssa had ever imagined.

What would she be without Will to fight with, to push off against? Would she just disappear?

"I mean — " She wasn't going to cry. No way. Not in front of Will. "I mean, coming right up." She ran for the water keg. "Anything you want, you just ask."

The twin-engine plane left first, carrying away Red Hair and his two colleagues. Mr. Big left on the second aircraft. By this time, his white suit was a mass of wrinkles and sweaty soil. If he was broken up by the death of his Doberman, he gave no sign.

Luke, J.J., and Charla watched from their usual spying place as the single-engine plane rose from the water, carrying its illegal cargo of tusks and animal parts to who knew where.

"Think they'll be back?" asked Charla.

"Count on it," said Luke. "This is the perfect meeting place for an exchange like that. Why do you think they needed to make sure there wasn't anyone here but them?"

After so many days of hiding, it felt almost unnatural to be able to run down the coral bluffs to the beach without fear of the smugglers. Luke kicked off a shoe and dipped his toe in the warm water of the lagoon. It was hard to believe that only a week had passed since they had witnessed Red Hair executing one of his own men in this very spot.

J.J. skipped a flat rock on the surface of the lagoon. "Well, we've got the run of the place now. We can throw wild parties. Too bad there's nobody to invite but a bunch of snakes."

"We can get rescued," Charla corrected pointedly. "This is our big chance until the smugglers come back. If we blow this . . ." Her voice trailed off.

Once again, Luke used the footprints on the beach as a guide to find the hidden military installation. Even though he'd been there before, the jungle was so dense that the Quonset hut was virtually invisible until the castaways were standing right in front of it.

J.J. stepped inside and looked around with distaste. "What a dump!" he said sourly. "Man, remind me never to join the army."

Charla's eyes were wide. "It's hard to believe that all this was here to kill people."

"There was a war on," Luke reminded her.

"Yeah, but one bomb — wiping out a whole city." She shook her head sadly. "It's scary what we've taught ourselves to do."

Luke noted that the sleeping bags were no longer on the benches. A newspaper lay folded over on one of the seats. He flipped it open. *USA*

Today, from July twenty-fifth — the day the first group of traffickers had arrived on the island.

Luke's jaw dropped. "Guys — "

There, at the top of the front page, was Mr. Radford, the mate of the *Phoenix*. The photograph showed him being pulled out of a battered dinghy by sailors on a Chinese freighter. As the others gathered around, Luke began to read:

HEROIC MATE FOUGHT IN VAIN TO SAVE KIDS ON SINKING BOAT

J.J. Lane, son of actor Jonathan Lane, is one of six youths lost at sea and presumed dead after the sinking of the *Phoenix*, the flagship of Charting a New Course, a renowned sailing program for problem kids. James Cascadden, 61, captain of the sixty-foot schooner, was also lost in the accident, which took place in near-typhoon conditions five hundred miles northeast of Guam.

According to Calvin Radford, 37, the only survivor, the tragedy began to unfold when Lane, 14, inexplicably tried to raise sails at the height of the storm. At that point, wind gusts up to seventy knots and forty-foot waves "tore the boat to splinters," according to Radford.

"He was a crazy kid — maybe Hollywood does it to them. But he didn't deserve to die like that," Radford said emotionally. "None of them did."

Luke Haggerty, 13, of Haverhill, MA; Charla Swann, 12, of Detroit, MI; Ian Sikorsky, 11, of Lake Forest, IL; and Will Greenfield, 13, and his sister, Lyssa, 12, of Huntington, NY, were the other victims.

Radford, the *Phoenix*'s mate, fought desperately to save the six young people after Cascadden was swept overboard by "a freak wave." It was only after the schooner sank out of sight that he climbed aboard the twelve-foot dinghy he would sail for eight days and more than two hundred miles before being rescued by the *Wu Liang*, a freighter out of Shanghai en route to Honolulu.

When called a hero, Radford broke down in tears. "Those kids were my responsibility! I should have found a way to save them."

The Maritime Commission has submitted his name for their highest medal for bravery.

Jonathan Lane could not be reached for comment, but according to spokesman Dan Rapaport . . .

Luke put down the paper, shaking with rage. "I'm speechless!" he seethed. "Rat-face — a hero! After what he did to us — "

"*Will*'s Rat-face had more heroism in his little

finger," Charla agreed emotionally. "You know, if boars have fingers."

J.J. shook his head. "My dad made a comment through a spokesman," he chuckled. "A *spokesman*! It's so totally like him that they almost had me fooled."

Charla stared at him. "What are you talking about?"

"If CNC could sink our boat and strand us on an island," the actor's son explained, "then it's definitely no big deal to print a fake issue of *USA Today*."

Luke waved the paper in his face. "They interviewed my *mother* about me being dead!" he seethed. "Is that real enough for you?"

"She's in on it," J.J. argued. "All our parents are. They're the ones who sent us to this Sleep-away Camp of the Damned."

Charla was furious. "I can't believe you're still talking about this! Poor Will's got a *bullet* in his leg! You think *that's* part of CNC's plan?"

"That must have been a mistake," J.J. said seriously. "It could be our ticket out of here. Sooner or later they're going to have to call the whole thing off to get Will to a doctor. We just have to hang tough."

"Oh, we'll hang tough, all right," Luke vowed. "But it has nothing to do with your idiot theories.

We're going to hang tough so we can live to tell the world what Rat-face did to us, and watch him rot in jail for it!"

Ian had asked them to bring back whatever medical supplies they could find in the hope that there might be something that would help Will. They came up empty in the main building, but one of the smaller huts in back turned out to be a dispensary. Loaded down with bottles, bandages, and sterile pads in yellowed packets, the three started out on the return journey to their camp on the other side of the island.

They had been walking for only a few minutes when, all at once, J.J. disappeared. One minute he was striding at the head of the group; the next, he was just *gone*.

"J.J.?" called Charla, mystified.

"Down here," came a strangely distant voice.

"Quit fooling around," Luke said sharply. "We've got to get this stuff to Will."

"No, really!"

A hand reached up and parted the thick underbrush. They stared. J.J. stood at the bottom of a large square pit, up to his knees in dirt and rotted leaves. Bottles and gauze pads were scattered everywhere.

"Is that supposed to be there?" asked Charla. "Like a trap or something?"

"Sure trapped me." J.J. shrugged, rubbing his head. "I think I fractured my skull."

Luke was impatient. "If the fall didn't break those bottles, I'm sure your thick head's okay too."

"There's something hard down here," J.J. insisted. He began kicking at the dirt of the pit. There was a dull clang, and he jumped back. "Ow!"

Luke frowned. "That sounded like metal." He eased himself into the hole and reached up to help Charla after him.

J.J. was already digging at the earth and leaves of a mound at the center of the pit. A few inches below the surface, he struck black metal with a smooth rounded surface.

The dirt came away easily, and the other three joined him in clearing off the strange object. It was huge — maybe ten feet long and far too heavy to budge. The thing resembled a very tall black garbage can with fins on one end.

"Let me guess," ventured J.J. "It's Chap Stick for giants."

Suddenly, Luke just knew. There was no flash of inspiration, no lightbulb going off in his brain. He simply looked at the object, and in that instant, realized exactly what it was.

Involuntarily, he took a step back.

"What's wrong?" asked Charla in concern. "All of a sudden, you're pale as a ghost!"

"I think — " Luke began shakily, "I think we just found Junior."

They goggled. Wide staring eyes moved from Luke, to the object, and then back to Luke again.

Charla was the first to speak. "You're not saying — ?"

Luke nodded weakly. "The Discovery Channel was wrong. They *did* build it. And they left it right here."

This time, everybody stepped backward. J.J. plastered himself against the wall of the pit.

A harsh reality dropped over the castaways like a smothering blanket. A hostile environment and dangerous enemies were only part of the problem. Their friend Will was beginning a fight for his very life. And now, thrown into the mix by some insane quirk of fate — an atomic bomb.